The Urbana Free Library

To renew: call 217-367-4057
or go to "*urbanafreelibrary.org*"
and select "Renew/Request Items"

ALREADY
GONE

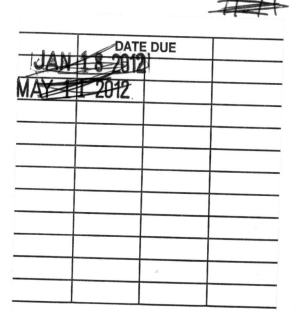

ALREADY
GONE

11-11

JOHN RECTOR

ALREADY GONE

A NOVEL

15 °°
10/11

Text copyright ©2011 John Rector
All rights reserved.

Printed in the United States of America.

Published by Thomas & Mercer
P.O. Box 400818
Las Vegas, NV 89140

ISBN-13: 9781612180878
ISBN-10: 1612180876

For Zoe and Eliot, with love

PART 1

− 1 −

I put up a good fight.

But once they get me on the ground, facedown, with the big guy holding my arms and pressing his weight into my back, there isn't much I can do. I call them every name I can think of, but they don't say a word. I tell them they can take my wallet, my car, anything they want, if they just get the fuck off me.

Still nothing.

I try to roll to the side, but the big guy grinds his knee into my spine and pulls up on my arms. My shoulder starts to slip in the socket and I scream, more out of frustration than pain.

Inside the bar, everyone is still drinking. Doug is telling stories about the sixties and getting high with the Beats, while the rest of the faculty listens and laughs and pretends to be impressed. I know this because up until five minutes ago, I was one of them.

Now I'm out here with these two, and I have no idea who they are.

I'd seen them earlier, sitting at the end of the bar and staring at our table, but I didn't think anything of it at the time. It was a quiet place, and Doug was loud. Everyone was staring. The only reason I noticed them at all was because of the jagged scar on the little one's neck. It ran from one ear to the other like a swollen pink worm, bright and impressive.

After a couple drinks, I told everyone I had to get home to my wife. There were a few good-natured newlywed jokes that I waved off before getting up to leave. Someone, obviously drunk, said we should have all our department meetings in bars.

Everyone laughed.

As I walked out, I didn't see the two guys at the bar, and I didn't notice anyone following me. Once outside, everything was quiet and dark. There was a soft breeze passing through the trees lining the parking lot, and the late summer air felt cool against my skin.

I took the keys from my pocket and started walking. I was almost to my car when I heard footsteps coming up fast.

I turned, but it was too late.

One of them hit me across the face, hard, and for an instant everything faded. Then the pain focused me and I started swinging. It was two against one, but I still managed to get in a few good shots before they took me down.

Now I'm here.

This isn't the first time I've been jumped, and since I don't see a gun, I figure everything will be okay. A few bruises, wallet gone, nothing I can't walk away from.

Then I see the bolt cutters.

"What the f—"

Again, I try to struggle free, and again the big guy presses down on my back, harder this time, and all the air rushes out of my lungs. I can't breathe, and an explosion of tiny black flowers blooms behind my eyes. I taste the oiled surface of the asphalt on my lips and try to lift my head to see what's coming.

Behind me, the big guy says something in a language I don't recognize, then the man with the scar and the bolt cutters steps closer.

I try to say something, anything, but there is no air and no voice. Dark shadows creep in along the edges of my vision, and I know I'm close to passing out.

My lungs burn.

I barely notice the big guy prying my hand open.

I bite the insides of my cheeks so hard I taste blood. It brings me back, just a little, but it's enough.

I won't let myself pass out.

I feel the cold metal blades slide around my finger, and I close my eyes tight.

I won't pass out.

A second later, the man with the bolt cutters leans forward. There is a quick, hard movement, and I hear something snap, loud and wet.

The pain is stunning.

It screams up my arm and into my brain and then it is everywhere and I forget all about my lungs. Again, the dark shadows rush in from the edges like a flutter of wings, blinding me, turning the world black.

This time, I let them come.

— — —

When I open my eyes, the big guy is standing over me wiping his hands with a small white towel. I'm on my back staring up at one of the streetlights in the parking lot. Hundreds of tiny bugs circle in the pale yellow glow. It makes me think of winter and snowfall.

The two men are searching the ground by my feet, ignoring me. A moment later, the one with the bolt cutters bends down and pushes my legs aside. When he stands, he's holding my severed finger by the tip.

The streetlight reflects clean and gold off the wedding ring just below the knuckle.

I want to stand. I want to tell them not to take my ring, but I can't find the words. I try to sit up, but the pain in my ribs pushes me back.

I don't have the strength to scream.

I stay on the ground and listen to the breath rattle in my chest. I have to cough. I try my best to hold it in, but I can't, and this time I do scream.

The big guy bends down and reaches for my hand.

I don't even try to fight.

He takes the white towel he was using and presses it against the spot where my finger used to be, then he takes my other hand and holds it against the towel.

"Tight," he says.

My left hand is warm and wet. I pull it in and squeeze it to my chest. The towel is red with blood.

The big guy stands and says something to the man with the bolt cutters. The man nods and starts walking across the parking lot.

The big guy watches him go, then looks down at me and says, "Nothing personal, okay?"

The accent is thick, and I can't place it.

"Fuck you," I say.

It isn't much, but it's all I have.

The big guy smiles, turns, and is gone.

I stay on the ground, unable to move, staring up at the pale yellow light. I think about Diane and about the wedding ring I've worn for the past month, the one I'll probably never see again.

All at once, I feel like crying.

I'm not sure why.

I put up a good fight.

- 2 -

"The good news is that it's a clean cut. You probably won't need surgery."

This is good news.

Anything is good news when you're on morphine.

My hand is resting on a silver suture tray and covered in a cocoon of white gauze that makes my arm look like an oversized Q-tip. The doctor examines the bandage, then puts a hand on my shoulder and says, "You're not a piano player, are you?"

I ignore him and turn toward the cop sitting on the red plastic chair next to the bed. He's talking to Diane, asking her if she knows of anyone who might want to hurt me. He wants to know if I have any enemies.

Diane is staring at the walls, the floor, her hands, anywhere but at him. There are tears on her cheeks, and when she speaks her voice is soft.

"No one," she says. "Of course not."

The cop looks at me. "How about you? Anyone out there holding a grudge?"

"A grudge?" Diane looks from me to the cop, then back. "Over what?"

The cop stares at me, waiting.

"No," I say. "I don't think so."

The cop scribbles something in his notebook.

"What is he talking about?" Diane asks. "Does someone want to hurt you?"

"No." I shake my head. "No one."

I can tell Diane wants to say something else, but instead she just frowns and looks away.

Nobody says anything for a while. Finally, Diane straightens in her chair and says, "So, what's the next step?" She reaches for my good hand, squeezes, then turns back to the cop. "How long before you find these people?"

The cop looks up, and to his credit he doesn't smile, but I can see it in his eyes.

He tells her once the report is filed, it'll be assigned to a detective who will go over the details of the case, talk to witnesses, run any descriptions through the database. He tells her they'll follow every lead to make sure the two men are caught.

If this were any other time, I'd laugh.

The cop will file a report. A detective might even look at the report, but that's where it'll stop. Random violence cases, especially the ones with no witnesses and no fatalities, are rarely solved.

I know this.

The cop knows this.

I think on some level Diane knows this, too, but we all go through the motions and play our roles. Who knows, maybe this will be the one time the system works.

— — —

Once the cop is gone, the doctor comes back with prescriptions for pain medication and antibiotics. He hands them to Diane and says, "Keep the hand clean and watch for infection. Make sure he takes the antibiotics. If you see anything strange, bring him in."

Diane tells him she will, and after he leaves, she sits next to me on the side of the bed.

"What did that cop mean about someone holding a grudge?"

"No idea."

"Is it because of your dad?" she asks. "You mentioned some of his friends in the book. You don't think one of them saw it and—"

"You're reaching," I say. "The two guys tonight were strangers, I've never seen them before. They were probably drug addicts who wanted my ring so they could pawn it."

"But they didn't take your wallet."

"No," I say. "They didn't."

"It's strange, Jake."

"It is what it is." I sit up, slow, and point to my coat. "Let's get out of here."

Diane helps me with my jacket. My ribs are wrapped tight, and my hand won't fit through the sleeve so we run the jacket under my arm like a toga. It looks ridiculous, and I can't help but smile.

Diane doesn't.

"I just don't understand why they came after you," she says. "There were a lot of people in that bar, but they waited outside for you. There has to be a reason."

"I was alone. That was enough."

"You think that's it?"

"What else could it be?"

Diane stares at me for a moment, then shakes her head and looks away. "I don't know."

I take her hand. "If you start looking for answers and asking, 'Why me?' you'll go crazy. They came after me because they saw me as an easy target, that's all."

"But it doesn't make sense," she says. "You had money, and they didn't take it."

"I wish they had," I say. "I hate to lose that ring."

"It was just a ring. We'll get another."

"We can't do that. It's bad luck."

Diane laughs, soft and delicate. "The first one wasn't exactly lucky, was it?"

"No," I say. "I guess it wasn't."

- - -

When we get out to the waiting room, I see Doug sitting in a chair by the window. His head is back and his mouth is open and he's snoring. The sound echoes.

"Has he been here all this time?" I ask.

"I guess so," Diane says. "He must've stuck around after he called me."

I don't remember how long I was in the parking lot. My only memory is of someone pulling me up by one arm, then sitting in Doug's backseat with him telling me to keep my hand over my head.

"You want to wake him up?" Diane asks.

I tell her to go ahead, and she does.

Doug opens his eyes and looks from Diane to me. When he sees my hand, he winces. "Shit, Jake, what'd they say?"

"Apparently, someone cut off my finger."

9

Diane looks at me, frowns.

Doug shakes his head. "Who knows, maybe it'll improve your typing."

"Always the optimist," I say.

Doug stands and grabs his coat and slides it over his shoulders. "What did the cops tell you?"

"That they're working hard, following every lead."

Doug nods. "Then I guess it's just a matter of time."

He winks at me.

I can't help but smile.

\- \- \-

The three of us cross the parking lot together. I feel fine, but Diane holds my arm every step of the way.

Doug is reminiscing.

"I never once locked my doors until I went to college, and you want to know why I started?" He doesn't wait for an answer. "Because people kept coming in and taking my dope. Never because of this shit."

"It's a different world."

"And one I don't understand," he says. "It's like I woke up one day and everything was off-kilter. Not a lot, but enough to where all the rules have changed."

"I think that's called old age."

"I never locked my doors growing up," Diane says. "Now, I never leave them unlocked."

"See, your wife agrees with me." He looks at her, asks, "Where did you grow up, hon?"

"Name a place. My father was in the military so we moved a lot, base to base mostly."

"Military bases are safer than cities," I say.

"Obviously, you've never lived on one."

"Not everyone grew up like you did, Jake. Some of us remember a time when you didn't need to look over your shoulder when you stepped outside." Doug points at my bandaged hand. "And this kind of thing was unheard of. If they wanted your ring so bad, why didn't they just make you take the goddamn thing off?"

"You see?" Diane pulls at my arm. "It doesn't make any sense."

"Tell you the truth," Doug says. "I've had enough. A couple more years teaching, and I'm done. I've got a little place on the beach in Mexico. All mine. It'll be me, a few drinks, and the waves."

"Sounds nice," Diane says.

"It's beautiful. I'll make sure to have the two of you down for a visit. You can see for yourself."

No one says anything else until we get to Doug's car.

"I'll talk to Anne Carlson about rescheduling the meeting," Doug says. "She won't mind, considering the situation."

"I don't want to reschedule."

"Why not?"

"I don't want everyone making a big deal out of this."

"It is a big deal," Diane says. "Take some time before you jump back into things."

"I don't need time off. I want to move on. As far as I'm concerned, this never happened."

"But it did happen. You can't just pretend it didn't."

"I'm not pretending, but I'm not going to let it stop my life either." I look at Doug. "I appreciate it, but I'll be fine."

"Your call." Doug unlocks the car door and gets inside. "If you change your mind, let me know. Anne Carlson and I go way back. She'll understand."

I tell him I will.

Diane and I step back and watch him pull out of the hospital parking lot and drive away. We walk to our car, and when we get there, I notice she's crying.

"You okay?"

She nods and fakes a smile. "I just feel so bad for you. You didn't deserve this."

"It could've been a lot worse."

This doesn't make her feel better, but I can't think of anything else to say that might, so I put my good arm around her shoulder and pull her close. She leans into me until the tears stop, and then we get in the car and drive home in silence.

Halfway there, I feel my hand start to pulse under the bandage, and I realize the morphine is wearing off. The pain is still far away, but I know it won't be for long.

I take it as a warning.

Things are about to get worse.

- 3 -

The package arrives with the morning mail.

It's small, about the size of a coffee can, and covered in packing tape. I pick it up off the porch and set it on the kitchen counter.

"Another gift?" Diane asks. "Who's it from?"

"No idea." I hold it up and turn it from side to side. We've been getting a few late gifts since the wedding, but this one's different. There's no card and no return address, just our last name written on the plain white wrapping. "How the hell am I supposed to open it?"

Diane takes out a pair of scissors from one of the drawers and says, "Let me try."

"I can do it."

She looks at my bandaged hand and pulls the scissors away. "You should let me. It'll be easier if I—"

"I'm not a goddamn child, Diane. I can do it." My voice comes out harsher than I'd intended, and I stop myself. "I'm sorry, I didn't mean…"

This isn't the first time I've snapped at her in the past few days. Since the attack, all I've done is lie around the house and work my way through the bottle of Vicodin they gave me at the hospital. The pills help with the pain, but they don't do a thing for the constant itch grinding up from the spot where my finger used to be.

It makes it tough to stay in a good mood.

Diane says she understands, but that doesn't make me feel good about it.

"I am sorry," I say.

Diane sets the scissors on the counter and walks out of the kitchen and into the living room, away from me.

I don't blame her.

I look down at the scissors, then at the bandage on my hand. I feel the anger building in my chest, and I push it away the best I can.

It's getting harder to do each time.

When I think I have it under control, I pick up the scissors and set them on top of the package, then go to the closet by the front door and grab my coat.

Diane comes around the corner. "Are you leaving?"

"Going for a walk," I say. "I need to get out of the house for a while, get some fresh air, clear my head."

She steps closer and puts her hand on my arm, then leans in and kisses me, soft. When she pulls away, her eyes never leave mine, and as always, I lose myself a little inside them.

"Don't beat yourself up," she says. "With all that's happened, everything you're feeling is completely natural."

I nod, but I don't buy into the "victim's trauma" theory, at least not in my case. All I want to do is move on, go back to the way things were before. Sometimes I think I can do it, but there's another voice, a dark voice, and it won't let me forget, no matter how hard I try.

"I'll be fine."

Diane smiles, touches my cheek, then turns away.

I open the front door and walk out into the afternoon.

- - -

When I get to the end of the driveway, I turn left and start toward the university. I don't know how far I'll get, but I plan on walking until I can start acting human again, however long that takes.

Luckily, it's a nice walk.

The sidewalks in our neighborhood are wide and lined with towering oak trees whose leaves drape green over the streets in the summer and cover the ground gold in the fall. The closer you get to the campus, the older the houses and the quieter the streets.

Quiet.

That's taken some time to get used to.

When Diane and I first met, I had a studio apartment a few blocks from the capitol. There was a rooming house next door and a bar across the street, and it was anything but quiet. It wasn't the worst place I'd lived, but you didn't want to be out walking after dark, either.

Diane wanted nothing to do with it.

She was working as a buyer for a local art gallery, and living in a condo downtown. We decided that if we were going to get married, we needed a bigger place in a better neighborhood, something we could grow into. So, after I took the job at the university, we started looking.

We fell in love with the first one we saw.

It was a small brick Tudor tucked into one of the oldest neighborhoods in the city. Not too far from the gallery, and within walking distance of the university.

It was perfect, and we put an offer on it that night.

We didn't move in right away. Diane was superstitious and didn't want to live together before we were married.

"We can wait a month," she said.

I pointed out that we'd spent almost every night together since we met, but she wouldn't back down. She wanted us to be married first.

If I said it made sense to me, I'd be lying, but you do what you do for love. In the end, taking a step back to catch our breath turned out to be a good thing. Up until then, things had been anything but slow.

The first time I saw Diane was at a reading Doug had arranged at the university. I'd published a short novel with the university press earlier that year, and I was being considered for a teaching position. Doug thought a reading would cement the deal.

Normally, I would've jumped at the chance, but not this time. My father had just died of a heart attack in prison a few weeks earlier, and the last thing I wanted to do was get up and read in front of a crowd. I tried to back out, but Doug was insistent, so I went along.

The reading went fine, and after I'd finished, I stuck around to sign copies of the book. Diane was one of the first to come up. She told me how much my story had touched her and how it'd given her the courage to let go of her past and start over again. She said the book made her feel like anything was possible.

We talked for a few minutes, but I don't remember a word of what we said. What I do remember is the easy way she brushed a loose strand of dark hair from her face, tucking it behind her ear in one smooth and fluid motion, then smiling up at me in a way that I knew would change everything.

It was impossible for me to pretend I didn't notice.

I signed a few more books that night, and talked to everyone who came up, but I kept looking for her. And when the crowd thinned and people drifted away, she was still there, waiting for me.

That was the first night.

A month later we were engaged.

For the most part, people were supportive. We were both adults, and since neither of us had living family, we didn't have to explain anything to anyone. In the end, it was just the two of us.

We were married by a judge on a Wednesday afternoon.

It was beautiful.

It still is.

– – –

I walk to the campus then turn around and head back. No one else is on the streets, and by the time I get home things don't seem so bad. When I open the door and go inside, I feel better than I have in days. Diane is sitting on the couch with a book open on her lap.

She looks up at me and smiles. "Feel better?"

I walk over and kiss her.

"What's that for?" she asks.

"For being here."

Diane rolls her eyes, then turns back to her book and says, "Think about what you want to do for dinner."

I go into the kitchen and pour myself a glass of water. I finish it, then take a beer from the refrigerator and drink half of it.

For a while, I stand at the sink and stare out the window at a pair of squirrels chasing each other through the backyard. I stay there until the beer is gone, then I drop the bottle in the trash and open two more, one for me and one for Diane.

On my way back to the living room, I pass the package on the counter. The scissors are still on top, right where I left them. I set the bottles down and go to work.

Whoever taped the box did a thorough job, and cutting into it one-handed turns out to be a challenge. After struggling for a few minutes, I manage to cut through one corner. I peel away tape in long strips until I'm able to open the top and look inside.

The box is filled with bubble wrap, and as I pull it away, I begin to see the outline of a clear glass jar inside. It's heavy, and there's a piece of stationery taped to the lid, blank except for the words "*From the desk of Thomas Wentworth*" printed along the top.

The name doesn't mean anything to me, so I drop the note on the counter, strip away the last of the bubble wrap, and hold the jar up to the light coming in through the kitchen window.

When I do, I almost drop it.

The jar is half-filled with a thick amber liquid that glows gold in the sunlight. My severed finger is floating inside, weighed down by the wedding ring just beneath the knuckle.

At first, my mind doesn't register what I'm seeing.

My finger looks shrunken, fake. The severed end is a shred of torn flesh that drifts back and forth in the dark liquid like pale seaweed surrounding a jagged nub of bone.

I stare at it for a long time, feeling my hand pulse under the bandage. When I finally set the jar on the counter and step away, all I can think is that I got lucky.

I got my ring back.

- 4 -

Diane isn't taking this very well, so after I hang up with the police, I sit next to her on the couch and put my hand on her leg.

She looks at me. "What did they say?"

"They're sending someone."

"When?"

"I don't know. Now, I guess."

Diane turns toward the window and stares out at the empty street, silent.

I want to tell her everything will be okay, but I can't do it. I can't pretend that what happened to me that night in the parking lot was a random act, not anymore. I'm being targeted, and we both know it. I owe her more than false comfort.

"I've been thinking about what you said in the hospital," I say. "About my dad and the people he knew."

Diane looks at me.

"I'll give the cops a couple names. Maybe they can come up with some answers." I pause. "I don't want you to worry. I'm going to find out who's doing this."

"How are you going to do that?"

"I'll call Gabby, see if he can ask around. Someone has to know something."

"Gabby?"

"If anyone can find out, he can."

"That's your solution?"

"Whoever's doing this, we can find them. We can end it with one phone call."

She shakes her head then turns away and runs her fingers under her eyes, wiping away tears. "Just let the police handle it, okay? Don't get involved."

"I'm already involved."

"You're also still alive."

"What does that mean?"

"It means you don't know anything about these people or what they're capable of doing. You're in way over your head, even with Gabby."

"I'm not scared."

"I am, Jake. I'm fucking terrified."

I start to argue, but she stops me.

"I can't stand by and watch you get hurt again, I can't do it."

"Nothing's going to happen to me."

"You don't know that."

"I'm not helpless, Diane. I can handle myself."

She hesitates, and the way she looks at me makes me feel like a boasting child. I want to argue, but then I think about how hard all of this has been hard on her, and I don't say anything. Instead, I reach out and put my arm around her shoulder.

She resists at first, then leans into me and whispers something I can't hear.

I ask her to tell me again.

She sits up and touches my bandaged hand. "What kind of person would do something like this?"

I can think of a few people who wouldn't blink at doing things like this, or worse, but I keep that to myself and say, "I don't know."

Diane folds into me, and a moment later the tears begin again. We sit like that for a while, and neither of us says anything for a long time.

\- \- \-

The field tech arrives ten minutes after the detective. He comes in wearing jeans and sandals and carrying a large black case over his shoulder. The detective, whose name is Nolan, motions him toward the kitchen.

"On the counter."

The tech nods then disappears through the French doors. When he comes back he's carrying the jar in a large plastic evidence bag.

He asks if anyone touched the item.

"Mr. Reese here is the only one." Nolan watches me over his wire-framed glasses. "Is that correct?"

"That's right."

He looks at Diane, then turns back to the tech and says, "Better get them both, just to be safe."

The tech opens his case and takes out a smaller, dark blue container and a pair of plastic gloves. He unsnaps the smaller container. Inside is an ink tray, a roller, and several fingerprint sheets. He lays them out on the dining room table and slips on the gloves.

Diane stares at him, then looks away.

Detective Nolan flips through the pages in his notebook. "So this name, Thomas Wentworth." He taps the paper with his pen. "It doesn't mean anything to you?"

It's the third time he's asked the question, and I tell him my answer hasn't changed.

"No need to get defensive," he says. "I'm here to help."

"How exactly?" Diane says. "All you've done is ask the same question again and again."

"Mrs. Reese, I know these questions seem redundant, but look at it from our point of view. If you knew how many people we talk to—"

I see the field tech wave me over. I get up, leaving Diane alone on the couch with Detective Nolan.

"I thought you could go first," the tech says. "It'll just take a minute."

"What's this for?"

"We need to distinguish your prints from anyone else's they might find on the jar. It's standard."

"Sounds reasonable." I hold out my bandaged hand. "I'll be the easy one. Only half the work."

The field tech smiles, but I can tell he doesn't know what to say. He runs through the fingers on my right hand, rolling them along the inkpad then across the paper. When he finishes, he hands me several Kleenex and thanks me.

"No problem."

Behind me, I hear Diane say, "But you're not doing your job. If you were, we wouldn't be sitting here. Those two men would be in jail." She stands, and her voice gets louder as she speaks. "Don't come here and act like this is his fault."

Detective Nolan holds up his hands. "Mrs. Reese, I never said anyone was at fault."

"Just do your fucking job."

She moves past him to the front door. I try to stop her, but she grabs her purse from the small table in the entryway and walks out.

I look back at Nolan. He's watching me.

"What the hell did you say to her?"

"Nothing." He shakes his head. "I asked if you had any enemies, that's it."

I look out the window in time to see Diane's car pull out of the driveway and disappear around the corner.

"Maybe I should've saved that question for you."

I let the curtain close, then turn back to the living room and Detective Nolan. "The cop at the hospital already asked me."

"Right, but it's been a while, and you've had time to think about it since then. I thought you might've remembered someone."

"Sorry," I say. "No one."

Nolan flips through his notebook. "I pulled your old file." He taps his pen down the page, counting as he goes. "Multiple assault and battery charges, disturbing the peace." He turns the page. "And an assault with a deadly weapon charge. A brick." He looks at me. "All street fights. Sounds like you had quite a temper."

"It was a bad neighborhood."

"Does your wife know about all these?"

"She knows."

"Are you sure?" He motions to the door. "Because it doesn't look like it to me."

I hear the smile in Nolan's voice, and all the muscles in my body get tight, ready to snap. I remind myself who I'm talking to and try my best to calm down.

"She knows about all of it."

"Then what else can you tell me?"

"You've got my file. It's all in there."

"It's never all in there." Nolan closes his notebook. "Look, Mr. Reese, I want to help, but I can't do much if you won't talk to me."

"That was another life," I say. "I put those days behind me a long time ago. And if someone from those days is coming for me, why did they wait so long?"

"You tell me."

I shake my head. "Isn't that your job to figure out?"

Nolan stares at me for a moment, and then he stands and takes a card from his jacket pocket. He holds it out to me and says, "Call if you think of anything that might help."

I don't take the card.

He drops it on the coffee table. "Tell your wife I'm sorry for upsetting her."

"I'll do that."

Nolan walks to the kitchen table where the lab tech is filling out forms. He leans in and says something I can't hear. The tech nods, then packs his case and slides it over his shoulder.

I hold the door open for them as they leave. Once they're outside I remember and ask about my ring.

"Your ring?"

"My wedding ring." I point to the evidence bag the tech is carrying. "On my finger, in the jar."

"What about it?"

"I want it back."

- 5 -

"Evidence," I say. "I can get the ring back when they send my finger off to medical disposal, whenever the hell that happens. Your guess is as good as mine."

Diane doesn't say anything.

She walked through the door about an hour after the cops left. Now she's sitting at the kitchen table picking over a bowl of butter noodles with a fork.

I watch her for a while, then say, "You think this is my fault, don't you? Something I did."

She looks up. "No, I don't."

"What'd that cop say to you?"

"He kept asking about you."

"Do you think I'm hiding something?"

"No."

"But you're not sure?"

Diane sets her fork down then reaches across the table and puts her hand on mine. "I know you're not. And I know that whatever this is about, you're not the one to blame."

"You're distant now."

"I know."

"Are you going to tell me why?"

She sits back. "I suppose I feel helpless, like I should be able to do something."

"That's it?"

"That's it."

I don't believe her.

I know Diane loves me, but this wasn't what she signed up for. She wanted to marry the kid she read about in the book, the one who pulled himself out of the fire, not the one still burning.

I hope I'm wrong, but something tells me I'm not.

– – –

Two days later, I go back to the doctor and have the Q-tip bandage replaced with a smaller one. The new bandage covers the fingers on the left side of my hand, leaving my thumb free. It's not much, but I can use my hand again.

We haven't heard from Detective Nolan, so on the third day, I call him. He tells me there were no fingerprints, other than mine, on the jar, the tape, or the packaging.

"So now what?" I ask.

He pauses, then gives me the stock answer: following every lead, no stone unturned.

My fault for asking.

"How about the two men who attacked me? Anything on either of them?"

"Not yet," Nolan says. "We talked to the bartender who was working that night. He remembered them, but didn't have much to add. Said they never talked, even to each other, and when they talked to him, he could barely understand a word."

"That helps."

"Did your wife make it back?"

"She did."

"No worse for wear, I hope."

"She's fine." I try to move the conversation away from Diane. "Will you call if you find anything else?"

"You'll be the first person I call."

\- \- \-

The next day Diane tells me she's leaving.

"Just for a couple days," she says. "I have to meet with a client in Phoenix who wants to sell part of his modern collection. We're meeting with his lawyer to go over the details. He has to sign some papers."

I'm used to Diane traveling for her job, but this time it's different. I want to ask her why she didn't tell me about this trip before now, but I don't.

I understand what's happening.

We drive to the airport, and I wait with her until the flight boards. Diane doesn't like to fly, so I keep talking, trying to distract her.

"My classes start this week," I say. "I think I'm ready, but I guess we'll see."

She nods, silent.

"There were still seats open last time I checked. That's not a good sign."

Diane looks at her watch, then back over her shoulder. She's not listening to me, so I decide to keep quiet until they start boarding her flight.

When it's her turn, she looks at me for the first time since we arrived, then leans in close and kisses me, long and soft.

I tell myself it isn't a good-bye kiss.

"I'll see you in a couple days," she says.

"Call me when you get to the hotel."

She stands and slides her purse over her shoulder then takes a deep breath. "I should've driven. If I'd gone through the mountains I could've made it to Phoenix in plenty of time." She smiles at me, but it doesn't touch her eyes. "Have I ever told you how much I hate flying?"

"You might've mentioned it a few times," I say. "But it'll be all right. It's a short one."

She nods, kisses me again. "Bye, Jake."

I watch her cross the terminal and hand her boarding pass to the ticket agent. Before she starts down the tunnel toward the plane, she looks back and waves.

I raise my hand. Then she's gone.

— — —

A couple days turns into a week.

Diane apologizes. She tells me her client and his wife are fighting over what pieces to sell, and the lawyer can't work up a contract until they make a decision.

I tell her it's fine, then ask, "How's Phoenix?"

"Hot, dry, and crowded," she says. "It's grown so much since the last time I was here. I'm not sure I like it anymore."

"Sorry to hear it."

"No, I'm being too negative. The hotel is gorgeous. I've got a row of palm trees right outside my window, so that's nice. I just wish you were here."

"Me too."

"I think I'll take a day and explore, maybe drive up north to Sedona. Spend some time having my chakras realigned or my aura polished or whatever else they do up there these days. I'll bring you back a crystal necklace."

"Sounds like fun."

"I'd rather be home." She pauses. "Hey, how did your class go? I forgot to ask."

"Not what I was expecting," I say. "Mostly business majors who signed up thinking it's an easy class."

"Is it?"

"Haven't decided, but there are a lot of things I'd rather do than grade essays."

"I don't blame you."

I look at my watch. "Speaking of class, I should go. My next one is about to start."

"Monday, then?"

"Monday." She's quiet for a moment, then says, "I love you, Jake. Very much."

It fills me.

"I know," I say. "I'll see you soon."

And for the first time since she left, I believe it.

− 6 −

I'm struggling to fit a stack of papers into my bag when I hear someone knock at my office door. I look up as Anne Carlson, the department chair, steps inside.

"Got a minute?" she asks.

"Sure, come on in."

This is the first time Anne has been in my office. I start to apologize for the mess, but she doesn't seem to notice so I don't point it out. Instead, I motion to the chair across from me and say, "Do you want to sit down?"

"No, thank you. I only wanted to stop by and see how you're holding up after your first week." Her eyes drop to my bandaged hand and the stack of papers. "Do you need help with those?"

"I think I do," I say. "You never realize how much you rely on both your hands until one is gone."

Anne smiles. She takes the papers and straightens them on the desk then slides them into my bag. "How's your hand healing?"

"Slowly, but it's getting better."

She nods, and I can tell my answer was irrelevant.

"Mr. Reese, I thought you should know that I got a call the other day from a Detective Nolan. He said he was investigating the attack."

"Why did he call you?"

"That's what I asked him. Turns out, he had a couple questions that needed to be answered. Questions about you."

I pause. "What about me?"

"He wanted to know if I'd noticed anything out of the ordinary. If you'd had any strange guests, missed a lot of work, that kind of thing."

"What did you tell him?"

"I told him the truth," she says. "I explained that this was your first year and I didn't know you well enough to decide if something was out of the ordinary."

"Did he say why he wanted to know?"

"Not directly, but I got the impression he thinks you're wrapped up in all this, and that what happened to you might've been a direct result of your involvement."

"My involvement in what?"

"He didn't give specifics."

"Of course he didn't." My voice comes out sharp, and when I speak again, I make an effort to stay calm. "I can't defend myself against baseless accusations."

"You think he's lying?"

"I think he's lazy," I say. "He's looking into my case, but since he doesn't have anything to go on, he's assuming I'm somehow to blame because of the trouble I got in as a kid."

"But your not?"

"Of course I'm not. Are you worried about it?"

Anne shakes her head. "No, Mr. Reese, and I apologize for putting you on the defensive like this. I hope you understand it's not something I enjoy. It's just the university isn't accustomed to police detectives investigating our staff."

I keep quiet.

"All I can go on is my instinct and your word," she says. "My instinct tells me to trust you and that this is all a misunderstanding."

"That's good."

"I can assure you, if you tell me you're not involved in anything illegal or in anything that might harm the reputation of the university, then I'll support you one hundred percent."

We stare at each other, silent.

"Can you tell me that?"

I smile. "I'm not involved in anything, illegal or otherwise, that might harm the reputation of this university."

She nods. "Thank you."

Behind her, there's a quick knock at the door, then Doug's voice. "Jake, you in here?" He looks in and sees Anne. "Sorry, I'll come back."

"It's okay, Doug," Anne says. "I just stopped by to check in on Mr. Reese, see how he's managing after his first week." She hands me my bag. "I hope you'll come to me if there's anything I can do to help."

I tell her I will.

She turns, and I watch her walk out.

Doug closes the door behind her and says, "Didn't expect that. What did I miss?"

I don't answer him. I'm thinking about what I'm going to say to Nolan the next time I talk to him. There are a few different ways I see it going, each one ending badly.

"Hey," Doug says. "What the hell happened?"

I sit and lean back in my chair. I still want to yell at someone, but not Doug. That wouldn't do any good; he's known me too long. If he reacted at all, he'd probably just laugh, and that would make things worse.

"The detective investigating my attack called and asked questions about me."

Doug nods. "She told you about that?"

"You knew?"

"I heard this morning." He sits in the chair across from me. "I was coming down to talk to you about it."

"A little late," I say. "I could've used a warning before she showed up."

"Don't worry about her, and don't worry about that detective. He's a cop, and they ask questions. It's what they do." Doug pauses. "Is there something else going on?"

"Something else?" I get up and slide my bag over my shoulder. "Like what?"

He shakes his head. "Forget it. If you wanted me to know, you'd tell me."

He's right, I would, and hearing him say it makes me wonder why I haven't come to him. Doug has been there for me since I was a kid, and there's nobody I trust more.

The first time we met, I was locked in the Summit Juvenile Detention Center outside the city where Doug had come to tutor a class in English and composition. He walked in with a stack of books and handed them out. The one he gave me was about a group of boys stranded on a deserted island. I never opened it in class, but when I got back to my room, it was waiting for me on my bed along with a note.

It'll set you free.

I sat down and read it, and over the next six months, I read every book he gave me. Some were better than others, but all of them made an impression.

Later, when I was in college and I told him I wanted to write a novel based on my life before I was arrested, he supported me every step of the way. Sometimes he offered advice, but mostly he just read the pages and encouraged me to keep going.

When the book was finished, he pushed me to submit the manuscript to the university press. I fought him at first. The book was mine, a way to let go of my past, but Doug didn't let up. After it was published, he put my name in for the open teaching position at the college.

Any way you look at it, Doug changed my life.

I start toward the door, then stop and say, "Do you want to get a beer?"

"Of course I do." Doug gets up and looks at his watch. "It is almost noon."

"Then let's go."

"What about Diane? Is she going to object to you drinking in the middle of the day?"

"She's in Phoenix."

"You don't say." Doug puts a hand on my shoulder. "In that case, my friend, I know the perfect place."

- 7 -

I let Doug drive, and I don't pay attention to where we're going until it's too late. When I see the sign, I have to laugh.

"You're kidding."

"Give it a shot," Doug says. "They've got a great buffet."

"The Body Shoppe? You're serious?"

Doug pulls into the parking lot and turns off the engine. "Trust me, the food is good. You'll like it."

The building is a one-level box, no windows, and the paint is weatherworn, peeling away in long strips. The sign out front shows the silhouette of a woman bending forward with a man kneeling behind her and lifting her skirt with a car jack.

"Do you come here a lot, Doug?"

"No," he says, drawing the word out. "Almost never."

"I was thinking of someplace quieter."

Doug looks at me. "What do you want to do? Sit in a booth at Applebee's and drink piss beer and eat fake ribs? Why don't you live a little?"

Live a little.

I look up at the sign and shake my head, then I follow Doug through the front door and into The Body Shoppe.

— — —

I decide right away that I'm not going to eat.

The air inside is heavy and thick and has that sour smell that only comes to a place after years without sunlight. The music is loud, and there are several dancers on stage, each one swaying back and forth in the swell of smoke like naked corpses dangling from the rafters.

Doug taps my arm then points to the far wall and a line of booths facing out toward the main stage.

"The buffet is back there," he says. "It might be quieter."

I follow him through the maze of tables toward a booth at the back of the room. A waitress comes by and asks us what we want.

"Beer," I say. "In a bottle."

"Me, too," Doug says. "A glass is fine."

Once she's gone, Doug leans into the seat and says, "It's a clean place, Jake. You can get a glass."

"I don't think I'll take the chance."

Doug shakes his head.

I glance up toward the line of dancers on stage.

It's a hell of a sight.

None of the girls look younger than thirty, not even close. What I see is a showcase of caesarian scars and stretch marks, bruises so deep even the red and purple stage lights can't hide them.

I stare at them for a while, then turn away.

"So, what's going on?" Doug asks. "What's the story with this detective?"

I'm not sure where to begin, so I start by telling him about the jar and my finger. Doug listens and doesn't interrupt.

When I finish, he says, "Jesus, Jake."

"This detective is worthless. He thinks I'm involved because of the trouble I got in as a kid."

"The fights?"

"He doesn't have anything else to go on. Meanwhile, I'm watching Diane slip away, and I can't do anything about it."

"That's bullshit. She loves you."

"That might not be enough."

"Is that why she's in Phoenix?"

"She said she had to go for business, but there's more to it." I lean forward and tap one finger on the table. "The thing is, I could end this today. One phone call to Gabby and it's over, all of it."

Doug watches me. "You're not considering calling him, are you?"

"Why not?"

"You really need me to tell you?"

"Someone out there is after me, and I have no idea why. The cops aren't doing a thing about it."

"Give them time."

"How much time?" I ask. "I can't walk out my front door without looking over my shoulder. My wife is scared. My marriage is falling apart. I can't sit around and wait for the police."

"It's playing with fire. Gabby will want something in return, and you know it."

"Not with me. He'll help if I ask."

Doug pauses. "Yeah, I guess he might."

"Doesn't matter anyway. I told Diane I wouldn't call him. She wants to leave it to the police."

"Good," he says. "I understand your frustration, but wait and see what happens. The cops might surprise you."

I laugh. "No, they won't."

The waitress comes over with our drinks. She sets them on the table, says, "Help yourselves to the buffet."

We both watch her walk away.

"You eating?"

"Not hungry. Go ahead."

"In a minute." Doug leans forward. "Listen to your wife, Jake. Trust her. She knows you, and she loves you."

"All she knows is what I put in the book, that's it."

"There's more?"

"Some."

"She never asked?"

"She wanted to know more about my dad. I told her what I remembered about him and about my mother's suicide. That's about it." I pick up my beer and take a drink. "We made a deal before we were married to keep the questions to a minimum."

"You two must like surprises."

"I'm not hiding anything from her. She read the book. The worst of it's in there."

"Then trust her," Doug says. "It's her love for you that's going to get you two through this, despite all your shortcomings. I know it."

"We'll see."

Doug slides out of the booth and motions toward the buffet. "Sure you're not hungry?"

"I'm sure."

Doug shrugs, walks around to the buffet.

I stay at the booth and think about what he said. I'm not sure if it's his optimism or if it's the beer, but a part of me feels better.

Diane and I have a good life. We're happy together. Everything that's happened might've put some pressure on us, but there's nothing that's going to break us.

We're going to be fine.

\- \- \-

By the time we leave The Body Shoppe, we're both drunk. The sun has dropped behind the mountains, turning them into a jagged black silhouette along the horizon, as if someone reached up and ripped away the bottom of the sky.

Doug is standing in the doorway, talking to the bouncer. I'm leaning against the building, watching the cars pass along the street, wishing I were home.

Neither of us is in any condition to drive, so we have the bouncer call a cab. Fifteen minutes later, it pulls into the parking lot.

The drive home is quiet. When the cab pulls up in front of my house, I look over and see Doug leaning against the door with his eyes closed.

I sit forward and hand the driver several bills and say, "This should cover getting him home."

Doug sits up. "What the hell, Jake?"

I tell him it's a therapist fee and not to argue.

For once, he doesn't.

I open the door and step out.

Doug leans over, stopping me before I close the door.

"I have an idea," he says. "Why don't you and Diane take off at the end of the semester? Go away for a while, reconnect. I'll give you the keys to my place in Mexico. It's right on the water. You'll love it. I haven't been down in a couple years, so I don't know what shape it's in, but—"

"Thanks, but I can't go anywhere right now. Maybe once all this is cleared up, but not yet."

"Okay." Doug nods. "Of course."

He holds out his hand and I shake it.

"Let me know when she get's back from Phoenix. I'll have you two over. We'll grill a chicken."

I tell him I will, then I close the door and watch them pull away. Once the cab is out of sight, I turn and walk up the driveway to my front door and go inside.

The house is dark and empty and feels too big for just me. I think about Diane and wonder what she's doing right now. Picturing her touches something raw inside me.

I set my keys on the kitchen table and take a beer from the refrigerator. I walk down the hall to my office. There's a copy of my book in the closet. I take it out and start reading somewhere in the middle, hoping it will spark some long-forgotten memory.

Instead, there's just the familiar sick feeling I get whenever I think back to those wasted days. I don't get far before closing the book and dropping it on the desk.

It's pointless.

I knew so many people back then, and hurt so many more. The only way I'm going to find out who's after me is if I call Gabby for help, and that's not an option.

I sit behind my desk until the beer is gone, and then I walk back to the kitchen. I open the refrigerator for another beer, but I change my mind and grab the bottle of Johnnie Walker Black from the cabinet above the sink. I pour a good-sized shot into the bottom of a small rocks glass and drink it in one swallow.

It burns in the best possible way.

I pour another on my way to the living room. It's been a long day, and the night is threatening to be even longer.

I'll take all the help I can get.

I sit on the couch and sink into the cushions. Outside, the wind picks up, and I hear the branches of our ash tree tap against the window.

A few minutes later, thunder, and eventually rain.

- 8 -

At first I think it's a dream.

Diane is in the house, standing across from me with her jacket folded over one arm. There is a suitcase at her feet, and she's smiling. She picks up my glass and the empty Johnnie Walker bottle.

"You look comfortable," she says.

I am, but I know I won't be in the morning.

I tell her this, and she laughs, then leans in close and presses her lips against mine.

"I love you, Jake. Some surprise this turned out to be, huh?"

The words don't sink in right away. Diane's skin is soft and smooth and achingly real.

"I miss you," I say.

"Good night, Jake."

She lets go of my hand, then turns off the reading light and slips away toward the stairs.

I tell her I'll see her on Monday.

"You never know," she says. "Maybe sooner."

- - -

The next morning I walk into the kitchen and head straight for the coffee. Diane is standing at the sink with her back to me. The empty Johnnie Walker bottle is next to her on the counter.

"Tell me you poured that out."

Diane laughs. "Sorry, that's all you."

"Jesus." I turn away and take a drink from my cup. The coffee is strong and hot and I feel it all the way down. "Can't believe I did that."

"Do you remember me coming in last night?"

"I thought it was a dream. If I'd known you were coming home early, I would've been in better shape. I don't know what possessed me."

"Doug Peterson, probably. He's a bad influence."

"How do you know I was with him?"

"You don't exactly have a long line of friends."

She's right, of course.

Diane comes up behind me and runs a hand along my back. "How are you feeling?"

I go through a mental list of every part of me that hurts and say, "I've been worse."

"Good." She leans in close. "Because I have plans for you tonight."

I look at her, hopeful.

"I thought we could go out, somewhere nice," she says. "It'll give us a chance to talk."

"About what?"

"About us and everything that's happened." She looks at me. "Don't you think that's a good idea?"

"Are you going to tell me you want a divorce?"

Diane flinches. "Of course not."

I stare at her, silent.

"Is that what you think?"

"I don't know what to think," I say. "When you left, I thought you needed time to make a decision about us."

"That wasn't the main reason, but you're right. I needed time to think." She leans against the counter and crosses her arms over her chest. "Sometimes it seems like we don't know anything about each other."

"I'm not hiding anything."

"But you don't tell me anything, either. I don't know anything about you, your family, none of it."

"There's nothing to know about my family. I told you what happened with my mom, and my dad was in jail more than he was out."

"What about you?"

"All that's in the book."

"Not all of it."

"No, but everything that matters is in there." I pause, say, "Look, I was an angry kid and it got me in a lot of trouble, that's it."

Diane watches me, silent.

"Is this what tonight is about?"

"Tonight is about us going out, having fun, and talking." She steps closer. "I miss you, that's all."

"You don't want a divorce?"

She smiles, shakes her head. "No."

"You sure?"

"Completely." Diane slides around me, then presses her lips against my ear and whispers, "But no more secrets between us. We're in this together."

Her voice fills me.

I put my arm around her and hold her close.

I won't let her go.

Never again.

— — —

That afternoon, Diane and I are sitting out on the deck watching the leaves fall when the phone rings.

"Ten bucks says it's Doug." I lean forward and push myself up from the chair. "He's probably calling to see if I made it through the night."

"Tell him we need to talk the next time I see him."

I laugh, then cross the kitchen to the phone and pick it up.

"Mr. Reese?"

I was wrong, it's not Doug.

"Yes."

"This is Detective Nolan. I hope I'm not catching you at a bad time."

His voice sounds far away, but cheery. It almost makes me forget the problems he's caused at the university, but not quite, and for a moment I feel the anger flare in my chest.

I manage to hold it back and say, "Not at all."

"Good, that's good."

I hear him pull the phone away from his mouth. There is a muffled sneeze, and when he comes back to the line, he sounds like he's talking through cotton.

"Damn cold," he says. "Kicking me when I'm down."

I keep quiet and wait.

"Listen, I won't keep you. I just wanted to touch base on the news."

"What news?"

"You didn't read the paper?"

"No, should I?"

"You probably wouldn't have seen it anyway," Nolan says. "They buried the damn thing."

"What happened?"

"Our mystery man was found last night, facedown in the river, shot in the back of the head."

"Mystery man?"

There is a rustle of paper. Nolan clears his throat and says, "Thomas Wentworth, forty-six, wife, two sons, both off at college back East. He was some kind of high-level executive, CEO type. I'm looking into it."

"Who killed him?"

"It looks like a random robbery. We found his wallet about thirty feet from his body. His ID was inside along with a few pictures of his family, but no cash or credit cards. He's got a tan line on his wrist, but no watch. They probably took that, too."

"You think it's the same guys who came after me?"

"The thought crossed my mind, but he's still got his wedding ring, and all his fingers."

"Are you making a joke?"

"Maybe I am." Nolan laughs. "You know what they say, laughter keeps you from screaming."

"I've never heard that one."

"I might've made it up."

I wait for him to go on. When he doesn't I say, "So what can I do for you?"

"Unless you can tell me anything about Mr. Wentworth, not much." Nolan clears his throat and coughs again. "But while I've got you on the phone, can you tell me where you were last night?"

"I knew there was more to this."

Nolan doesn't speak.

"I got home around nine. I was alone."

"You got anyone who can verify that?"

"Nope."

"Where was your wife?"

"On a plane coming in from Phoenix."

"What's in Phoenix?"

"None of your business."

Nolan sighs. "Anyone at all know you were at home?"

"After nine? Not really. The cab driver who dropped me off. Doug Peterson, I suppose."

"Dropped you off?"

"Doug and I went out for a few drinks after work. We ended up taking a cab home."

"That's very responsible of you."

I open my mouth to start a fight, but I stop myself and say, "Anything else I can help you with?"

"Not unless something comes to you," he says. "You have my number."

I hang up and walk back outside.

Diane watches as I cross the deck to my chair.

"Who was it?"

I tell her.

"He was checking in," I say. "Still no leads on my case."

"Why am I not surprised?"

I don't say anything else.

We agreed, no more secrets, but I can't bring myself to tell her about the police finding Thomas Wentworth's body. I have no idea how she'll take the news, and I don't want to take the chance that it'll upset her again.

Right now, she's home and we're happy.

I'll do whatever it takes to keep it that way.

– 9 –

Over the next few weeks, life starts to return to normal. The doctor removes the bandage on my hand, revealing a thin, crescent-shaped scar and a smooth layer of skin where my finger used to be. He asks be about a prosthetic finger, but I tell him I'm not interested.

I've never minded scars.

Faculty meetings, classes, and student conferences take up almost all my time. I don't get to see Diane as often as I'd like, and that wears on us both. She says she doesn't mind, that she understands, but it's not true.

She does mind. We both do.

One Tuesday after class, I call home. I let the phone ring several times, and I'm about to hang up when Diane answers. She is out of breath, but her voice sounds warm, and I feel my day melt away as she speaks.

"What were you doing?"

She tells me she was out back, cleaning the garden.

"I wanted to get to it before the snows come," she says. "I barely heard the phone. I didn't think I was going to make it."

"I'm glad you did."

"It was close." She pulls the phone away, coughs, then she's back. "I almost killed myself on the steps."

I laugh, but she doesn't think it's funny.

We talk for a while. I tell her about my classes, and she tells me about her plan for the garden next year. I can hear the excitement in her voice and it makes me smile.

"Do you want to help? We can do it together. It'll be our project."

"You don't want me anywhere near your garden," I say. "I have a black thumb. Everything I touch dies."

"You just don't want to do the work."

"I'll help if you want, but you'll regret it." I turn toward the window and look out over the campus and the slow thread of students passing below. "Just don't say I didn't give you fair warning."

"Consider me warned," she says. "But all it takes is a little patience. You'll be fine."

"We'll see. Patience isn't my strong—"

There's a pause, then Diane says, "Are you there?"

I don't answer her.

I barely hear her.

I lean against the windowsill and focus on the two men sitting on the bench in front of my office. The big one, leaning back with his hands behind his head, and the little one next to him, wrapped in a khaki army coat. It's the first time I've seen them since the night in the parking lot, but I have no doubt it's them.

Diane asks me again if I'm there.

This time I find my voice.

"I have to go."

"What?"

I move away from the window and say, "I have to call you back."

"Why? What's going on?"

I hesitate before I say anything, and that gives me away. Diane can tell when I'm hiding something, and she asks again.

This time, I tell her the truth.

"Are you sure it's them?"

"It's them," I say. "I'm going down there."

This makes things worse, and the next time Diane speaks, I can hear the panic in her voice.

"Jake, don't."

"It's okay. I just want to talk."

"What?"

"They're right outside my office. What do you want me to do, pretend they're not there?"

"Call the police. Let them handle it."

"Like they've handled it so far?"

"Please." The panic is fading from Diane's voice, replaced by sadness, deep and tired. "Don't go down there, Jake. Promise me."

I walk back to the window and look out.

They're still out there.

"Goddamn it, Diane."

"Jake, promise me."

I stare out at the two men and try to stay calm.

"Jake?"

A group of girls walks by, and the big guy leans in and says something to the little one in the army coat.

He laughs, and I hate him for it.

"Jake, answer me."

Diane is crying now, and it brings me back.

"All right," I say. "I'll call the police."

Diane is still crying.

"I thought this was over. I'm sorry."

"It's not your fault."

But it is, and we both know it.

Something long buried is worming its way back into my life, our life. I don't know who's behind it, but I'm going to find out.

Just not today.

Today, I'm going to call the police.

"I want you to promise me something, Jake."

The tears are gone, but the sadness is still there.

"What's that?"

"Promise me you won't get carried away," she says. "Promise me you won't do anything stupid."

"What are you talking about?"

"Just promise me," she says. "Promise me you'll control your temper."

"Jesus, Diane, I told you I'd call the police and I won't go down there. What else do you want?"

"I want you to promise me."

"Fine, I promise."

Diane is quiet.

I'm about to tell her I need to get off the phone if I'm going to call the police, but she speaks first.

"I love you, Jake."

There's something in her voice that I don't like, something final, and I start to worry.

"Listen, I'll call the police and come straight home. We can talk when I get there, okay?"

No answer.

"We'll laugh about all this someday. You'll see."

Diane pauses. "Just remember your promise."

"Diane, I—"

The line clicks, and she's gone.

I stand there for a moment, staring out the window with the phone pressed against my ear. Then I walk back to my desk and set the receiver in the cradle.

I hesitate before I pick it up again and dial the number for the police. I go through all the right steps, just like she asked. It's not how I want to handle it, but I gave my word.

The police haven't been able to do anything, and I don't see that changing this time.

And I'm right.

By the time the police arrive, the two men are gone.

- - -

After the police leave, I walk home. I keep an eye out for the two men the entire way, but there's no one outside. The streets are deserted. The only sounds come from the wind and the scatter of dead leaves shuffling across the sidewalk as I pass.

When I get close to my house, I see that Diane's car is gone, and something inside me falls away.

I force myself to keep moving, but each step feels heavier than the last. I want to believe she parked in the garage today, but I know it's not true.

She's gone.

The front door is unlocked, and I push it open and step inside. The house is quiet. I call Diane's name, but there's no answer.

I let the door close behind me, then I walk into the kitchen and look out the window toward the garden at the far end of the lawn. Several yard bags are lying on the grass, and there's a rake leaning against the alley gate, but there's no sign of Diane.

I call her name again.

Still nothing.

I walk out to the hall and open the door leading to the garage. My car is inside, but Diane's is gone. Even though I'm not surprised, I don't move for a long time. I tell myself she just went out and that she'll be back any minute, but I know it's not true.

I close the garage door, then walk back to the kitchen and search for a note. I check all the obvious places, but there's nothing.

My thoughts roll over each other, one after another, and I can't keep them straight.

If she left, where did she go?

I head down the hall to our bedroom and go straight for her closet. Diane's clothes are inside, hung in a row. I push them aside, looking for her suitcase. It's on the floor, right where it's been since she got back from Phoenix.

I feel some of the tension inside me melt away, and for the first time that afternoon, I smile.

If she didn't pack, she didn't leave.

All at once, the world seems lighter.

I run my hand along the line of her clothes, feeling the fabric, soft and smooth under my fingers. I look for something I've seen her wear before, something I can attach a memory to, but nothing looks familiar.

It doesn't matter.

She didn't leave, and that's all I need to know.

I'm still smiling as I close the closet door. And even though my breath catches in my throat when I see the dark spots on the carpet, all bad thoughts are still a long way off.

It's not until I bend down and touch one of the spots with my fingertip, pulling it back wet and red, that those far away thoughts come screaming forward, tearing into my mind and closing off the entire world.

- 10 -

Detective Nolan holds up one hand and says, "Mr. Reese, you have to calm down."

We're standing in my bedroom and I'm pointing at the blood on the carpet, and all I can think is that he just doesn't get it, and that if I yell louder then maybe it'll click and he'll understand. Maybe he'll see.

But I don't yell.

I tell him again, calmly, "My wife has been kidnapped."

He pauses before he speaks. I know the technique. Cops use it to slow the conversation and release tension. The fact that I know what he's doing makes it even harder to stay calm. I turn away and start pacing the room.

"Did you check the doors and windows in the house?"

"For what?"

"If a lock is broken or if a screen door has been cut, then we'll have an indication that someone might've broken into your home. If that's the case, then we can explore the possibility that your wife was kidnapped."

"The possibility?"

Nolan's shoulders sag. "What do you want me to say?"

I feel the anger coming on strong, and I bite it back. "I don't want you to say anything to me. I want you to find her."

"We don't know she was kidnapped," he says. "All we have are a few spots of blood that could've come from anywhere or anyone."

"I told you, the two guys who attacked me, I saw them this afternoon. They were sitting outside my office, just down the street."

"You also told me your wife was upset." He looks at me. "This wouldn't be the first time she left because she was upset."

I open my mouth to argue, but I can't.

He's right.

"Give her some time," Nolan says. "I'm guessing she'll come home as soon as she calms down."

"And if she doesn't?"

"Then call us," he says. "But we can't open a missing-persons report for twenty-four hours. And without solid evidence, there's nothing we can do right now."

"What about the blood? Or her clothes?" I open the closet doors. "They're all here, same with her suitcase. If she'd left on her own, she would've packed a bag. She didn't take anything."

"Just her car."

I look away and don't speak.

"You'd be surprised how often people walk out of their lives with just the clothes on their backs," Nolan says. "A lot of times, people don't even know they're leaving until they're already gone. They grab their keys on the way to the store or maybe to work, and the next thing they know they're three hundred miles away. Something inside them just snaps."

"Not Diane."

"Maybe not," Nolan says. "But people do strange things when they're under stress."

He waits for me to say something else. When I don't, he motions in the air with his finger and says, "I'll take a look outside and see what I can see, but my advice to you is to stay by the phone and wait for her to call."

I walk Nolan to the front door, and he circles the house, checking the doors and windows. When he's finished, he cuts through my yard to his car.

I watch him pull away and wonder why I bothered.

– – –

After my third drink, I set the empty glass on the counter and stare out the window at the fading light and the evening shadows sliding long across the yard.

Diane hasn't called.

I reach for the Johnnie Walker bottle and refill my glass. I tell myself it'll be my last, then I walk out of the kitchen and into the living room. None of the lights are on, and for a while, all I can do is stand in the dark and listen to the silence of the house.

When it gets to be too much, I head down the hall to the bedroom and start searching through Diane's things. I have no idea what I'm looking for, but I have to do something.

I start with her dresser, searching through clothes and jewelry. Then I move to the closet and pull down a stack of boxes. I can tell there's nothing inside from the weight, but I still go through each one just in case.

When I finish, I put everything back, then take Diane's suitcase and open it on the bed.

It's empty.

I start checking the side pockets. All I find is a business card with a silver crescent moon and several blue stars embossed on the front. Printed underneath, in a clean gold script, is the name LISA BISHOP, and the word PSYCHIC.

I turn the card over.

There's an address and phone number printed on the back along with a handwritten note that says, "*D, we need to talk. Call me.*"

I put the suitcase back in the closet and walk out to the living room. On the way, I grab the phone and dial the number on the card.

I let it ring into voice mail.

Flutes and harps followed by a woman's voice, thanking me for calling, then asking me to leave a message.

I don't.

I hang up, then sit back on the couch and let myself sink into the cushions. I close my eyes and try to make sense of what I found.

On our first date, I took Diane to a French restaurant downtown. While we were in the bar waiting for our table, I told her it felt like we'd been there before.

I called it déjà vu.

She called it a chemical imbalance.

"Your brain is hiccupping and registering the present as a memory," she'd said. "No big deal."

That was Diane.

And that Diane would never go see a psychic.

I finish my drink then get up and pour another. I don't care if I get drunk. I want to get drunk.

There are too many questions, and I can't get my head around them. I can't focus. I keep seeing the two men sitting outside my office, and my thoughts keep returning to the same place, over and over.

Did they take her?

How could I have been so stupid?

They knew where I worked, so of course they knew where I lived. I could've told Diane to get out of the house, to run, but I didn't and now she's gone.

I take a drink and try to stop my imagination before it spins out of control. I focus on the cold ache in the center of my chest, letting it seep into the warm alcohol buzz, until the ache is all that's left.

Then anger.

I walk down the hall to my office and open my desk drawer. I take out my address book and flip through the pages until I find Gabby's number. I carry it back to the couch and pick up the phone.

I dial the first few numbers and stop.

I hear Diane's voice in my head telling me not to do anything stupid, and for a moment I'm able to convince myself that calling Gabby isn't stupid at all.

Then the moment passes.

If I'm going to bring Gabby in on this, I have to be sure. Once I make the call, whatever happens, I won't be able to take it back.

I stare at the phone in my hand for a long time, then reach for my drink and finish it.

Promise me you won't do anything stupid.

In the end, I don't make the call.

A promise is a promise.

– 11 –

I don't sleep for a long time. Instead, I lie in bed and stare at shadows and think about Diane. Eventually I drift off, and when I do, I have the dream again.

It's always the same.

In it, I'm a child, stacking building blocks on a dark carpet, watching them fall. My mother is in the next room, crying. She comes out and sits next to me.

I keep stacking the blocks.

"Jake," she says. "I want you to listen to me."

I look up at her and wait.

"You don't have to be afraid, do you understand?"

I nod and tell her I do, even though I don't.

She smiles, leans forward, and kisses my head. "Don't ever be afraid, Jake, not ever."

I watch her get up and walk into the bathroom, closing the door behind her. I wait, but she doesn't come out.

Eventually, I follow.

I stand outside, listening to the slow drip of the faucet, and then I reach out and push the door open.

I see her, lying in the tub, staring up at the ceiling. Her skin is blue, the water deep and red. There's a razor on the floor, and the light from the window flashes sharp along the edge.

The phone rings, pulling me back to the world.

"Jake, where are you?"

It's Doug. His voice sounds tired.

"You missed your first class," he says. "And your second is on the way out. What the hell's going on?"

I roll over and look at the clock on the nightstand.

It's past ten.

"Shit, Doug. I can't come in today."

"What?" He pauses. "What happened?"

I tell him Diane is gone.

"She left?"

"I don't know." I tell him about seeing the two men outside the office, then add, "I don't know what to think."

"What did the police say?"

I fill him in on my conversation with Nolan.

"They won't do anything for twenty-four hours, and since she's left before, they don't seem too concerned."

"But her clothes are still there," Doug says. "She wouldn't leave without packing."

"I know, and I told them the same thing."

"So what did they say?"

"Nothing," I say. "They just want me to wait by the phone in case she calls. I'm sorry I didn't let you know."

"You do what needs to be done. I'll post a note on your door. I wish there was something I—"

I stop him, not to be rude, but because there's nothing he can do to help.

"Thanks, I'll let you know."

When I get off the phone, I feel a low ping of dread deep in my chest. All I can think about is Diane and where she might be.

I play out several different scenarios in my mind, each one worse than the last.

It's not long before I can't take it anymore.

I get up and walk out to the kitchen and pour a glass of water. I drink half of it, then fill the glass with what's left of the Johnnie Walker and drink that, too.

The alcohol takes the edge off my headache, and for that I'm grateful. I set the glass in the sink, then walk back to the bathroom to take a shower.

By the time I finish, I almost feel alive again.

– – –

I dial the number, then flip the business card over in my hand and run my thumb along the blue stars embossed on the front. The phone rings twice. A woman answers.

I ask to talk to Lisa Bishop.

"Speaking."

For a second, I don't say anything. I didn't plan this far ahead, and I stumble over my words. Eventually, I recover enough to introduce myself.

"I'm not sure you can help me," I say. "I'm looking for my wife."

"Would you like to schedule a reading?"

"No, nothing like that. I think my wife was one of your clients, and I was hoping you could help me track her down. Her name is Diane Reese."

Lisa doesn't say anything.

I look at the business card. "She had one of your cards in her suitcase. I think she came to see you a few weeks ago. She was in Arizona on business, and—"

"What was the name again?"

I tell her.

"I'm sorry, it doesn't sound familiar."

"But she had your card."

"I'm afraid those cards are scattered around town like leaves. She could've picked one up almost anywhere."

"You wrote a note on the back." I flip the card over and read it to her. "You have to remember her. She's about five-five, dark hair?"

"I can check my journal if you'd like, but I remember everyone who comes to see me."

"Would you mind?"

I lean against the counter and listen to her shuffle through papers on the other end of the line. She's quiet for a while then says, "When did you say she was here?"

I give her a set of dates.

Lisa repeats them back to me, absently, then I hear pages turn, one after another.

"I keep accurate records of every reading I do, and I don't have anything for her. I'm sorry."

"But the note on the card says to call you."

"Someone else must've written it."

"This is the only phone number."

Lisa tells me again that she's sorry.

I feel a dull pain build behind my eyes, and I reach up and press my fingertips against my forehead.

It doesn't help.

"We can schedule a reading, if you'd like. It could provide some insight into the situation, maybe show you another path you haven't considered—"

"I don't need a goddamn reading." My voice comes out harsh, but I don't care. "I need to know what you talked about, if she said anything important."

Lisa pauses. "Mr. Reese, even if I had met with your wife, I wouldn't be able to tell you what we talked about. That's personal information."

"Let me guess, psychic–client privilege?"

Lisa sighs. "I believe it's more spiritual than that, but yes, you have the right idea."

The pain behind my eyes begins to glow, and I feel the muscles in my chest get tight.

I force myself to breathe.

When I'm sure I'm not going to yell, I say, "Listen, you're all I've got. My wife is missing, and I need to find her. She has no family, no close friends. All I have is your card and—"

"Mr. Reese, I—"

"No," I say, my voice growing louder. "Don't do that. Don't brush me off."

"But I don't know your wife. Do you understand?"

From there, the conversation goes bad.

It ends with Lisa hanging up and me standing in the kitchen, screaming into a dead line.

- 12 -

I spend the rest of the day finishing off the beer in my refrigerator. It helps with my headache, and for a while I don't feel too bad. It's not until I call Nolan and open the missing-persons report that I start thinking about something stronger.

The sun is going down, and the house is turning dark. I toy with the idea of walking down to the campus liquor store and picking up a bottle, but I don't want to be away from the phone, just in case.

Eventually, things get worse, and I grab my coat from the closet and force myself to leave.

The wind outside is cold and cuts against my skin. I zip my coat tight around my neck as I walk. There are no cars on the street until I get to the university. Then they are everywhere.

I can't take another step.

I stand on the side of the street, unable to move. My knuckles ache from squeezing my hands so tight. I pull them out of my pockets and massage the pain away, then I cross over to Main Street and cut through someone's yard, heading north toward Fifth Avenue.

There's a party in one of the houses up ahead. I see several people standing outside on the porch, shouting and laughing. When I get close, I hear glass shatter, then more laughter.

I keep walking, head down, trying to stay calm.

Fifth Avenue is at the end of the street, and I can see the liquor store on the corner. There's a crowd out front, students mostly, all smoking and talking, sitting on the sidewalk, leaning against the building.

I don't look at them as I walk by.

The chances of running into one of my students is slim, but it's a chance I don't want to take.

Once inside, things get worse.

The liquor store is tiny and crowded. People move through the lanes in loud groups, talking and laughing and turning the air stale.

I stay focused.

I know exactly where I need to go.

I weave my way through the crowd and grab a bottle of Johnnie Walker Black off the shelf then head to the counter at the front of the store. I get in line behind an older couple and wonder if they feel as out of place as I do.

The line inches forward.

To my right, the front door opens and several girls come inside, followed by an equally excited group of boys.

I reach for my wallet.

The couple in front of me is buying two bottles of red wine. They are both well dressed, and from behind they look respectable enough. I wonder how I must look with my uncombed hair, the dark circles under my eyes, and the yeasty, wet smell of stale beer on my breath.

I decide I don't care.

The line moves, and the couple in front of me buy their wine. When they turn to leave, I step forward and set the Johnnie Walker bottle on the counter.

"Mr. Reese?"

It's a woman's voice, and when I look up, Anne Carlson smiles back at me.

At first I don't say anything. I haven't spoken to Anne since she came to my office, and seeing her makes me realize there are worse people to run into than students.

I'm not sure what to say.

Luckily, she speaks first.

"You were behind us this entire time and I didn't even recognize you." She turns to the man she's with and says, "Walter, this is Jake Reese, one of our new instructors."

Walter holds out his hand and says, "Yes, of course. Nice to meet you, Jake. I read your book."

I shake his hand and thank him.

"And I knew your father," he says. "Well, I met him once. I did some work on his case before he passed away."

The clerk scans the bottle and gives me a price.

I hand him my credit card.

"Walter is an attorney with the city," Anne says. "We were on our way to a dinner party." She looks down at the bottle of Johnnie Walker on the counter and fakes a smile. "Big plans tonight?"

I open my mouth to tell her, no, just a typical Wednesday night, but thankfully Walter interrupts before I get a word out.

"I have to say, I don't know how much of it was true, but it was fascinating to read about your life, and your father's. He was an interesting man."

"I suppose he was."

"What did he do?" Anne puts a hand to her mouth. "I'm sorry, that was rude."

I shake my head and tell her it's okay. "He hijacked a truck. The entire thing was caught on a surveillance camera."

"By himself?"

"There were other people involved, but he was the only one who stepped in front of the camera."

"That's bad luck."

"That's alcohol," I say. "They knew where the cameras were mounted. He just got sloppy."

The clerk puts the bottle in a brown paper bag and hands it to me along with my receipt and a pen.

I sign my name, then walk out with Anne and Walter.

Once outside, I do my best to smile. I tell Walter it was nice meeting him and that I hope they enjoy their dinner party.

As I turn away, Anne stops me.

"Did you walk here, Jake?"

I motion down the street and say, "I'm close."

"Why don't you let us give you a ride? It's getting colder out here by the minute."

"I don't mind the walk."

"Come on," Walter says. "We insist, really."

I look down the street in the direction of my house. The cold doesn't bother me, but the idea of walking down those dark streets tears at me.

I decide to cut my losses.

"Thanks," I say. "A ride would be great."

I follow them around the liquor store to the parking lot. On the way, Anne asks about my classes and how the semester is shaping up. I tell her things are moving along, which seems to make her happy.

When we get to the parking lot, Walter presses a button on his keys, and the lights flash on a Mercedes next to us.

"Anne did say you worked for the city, right?"

Walter smiles, doesn't answer.

Anne sits in front, and I climb in the back. The seats are leather and soft. It's like sitting on kittens.

Walter asks if I'm comfortable.

I laugh, tell him I'm fine.

He pulls out of the parking lot and onto the street. "Where am I going?"

I lean forward. "Take a right up here, then a left about a mile down. I'll tell you when."

After a few blocks, Walter looks back at me in the rearview and says, "I hope you don't mind me saying something, but Anne told me about what happened." He pauses. "About the attack, and your finger."

I glance down at my hand. "It's in the past."

"That's good to hear." He reaches up and pulls a white business card from a clip on his visor and hands it to me over his shoulder. "But take this, just in case."

"In case of what?"

"In case it's not," he says. "You might want someone to talk to if they ever catch the guys, and I'll be happy to help out in any way I can."

I start to tell him he's wasting his time, but instead I pocket the card and remind myself that he's still my boss's date, and I need to be nice.

"Thanks," I say. "I appreciate it."

"Call anytime. I mean it."

We don't say anything else until we get to my street. I tell him where to turn, and as we come around the corner toward my house I say, "Third one from the—"

I stop. No one says a word.

Detective Nolan's cruiser is sitting in my driveway.

Walter pulls up in front of the house.

"Is everything okay?" Anne asks.

It takes me a moment to find my voice. When I do, I tell her everything is fine, even though I know better.

I grab my bottle off the seat and open the door.

Walter says, "Call me if you need anything."

I barely hear him.

I close the door then step up onto the sidewalk.

Detective Nolan is sitting on my porch. When he sees me, he gets up and starts across the lawn to where I'm standing.

I don't move.

Walter pulls away, slow, and I watch them until their red taillights disappear around the corner. I watch them because I don't want to look at Nolan.

I know what's coming.

The dead leaves on the lawn hiss under his feet as he walks. Then there's silence, and he's in front of me.

"Mr. Reese?"

Now I look at him.

I see it in his face, and I'm sure he sees it in mine. I wait for him to say something, and I don't wait long.

He says, "I'm sorry, Jake."

- 13 -

I'm riding in the passenger seat of Nolan's cruiser with the bottle of Johnnie Walker on my lap. I don't know where we're going, and I don't ask.

All I know is I'm supposed to identify Diane's body.

When I saw Nolan outside my house, he tried to tell me what had happened, that Diane had been in a car accident. When I didn't respond, he stopped talking.

I wasn't ready to hear about it.

Now I am.

"Her car went off the road on highway one sixty. It happened late last night, and no one found the vehicle until this evening."

I don't say anything.

"She must've fallen asleep while she was driving, probably on her way to Arizona."

"How do you know she was going to Arizona?"

"I don't," Nolan says. "But that's where the road leads, so I assumed—"

"Who reported it?"

"A retired couple was hiking through the canyon and saw the car. It doesn't look like anyone actually witnessed the accident."

I nod, not surprised.

"The rescue team took her to the county coroner in Fairplay. We'll see her there, then I'll drive you home." Nolan looks at me, then back at the road. "There was nothing anyone could've done. It was just an accident."

"You believe that?"

Nolan hesitates, says, "Don't, Jake."

"Do you believe that?"

"Yes, I do." He looks at me. "I believe this was an accident, because that's what it was."

I take the bottle from my lap and break the seal.

"Not in here," Nolan says.

I stare at him. "Are you kidding?"

He frowns, doesn't speak.

I take a drink.

Soon the city lights are behind us and the road narrows. We follow it into the mountains. I stare out my window at the endless blur of passing pine trees, dark against the darkness.

We don't say anything else, and by the time we get to Fairplay I've put a good-sized dent in the bottle, and I can feel it.

Nolan turns off the highway and drives through town. All the shops are closed, and the light from the streetlamps reflects white against black windows. There are a few couples outside, walking slowly along the sidewalks, hand in hand.

The county building is at the end of the street, tucked out of sight behind a line of aspen trees. There are no lights in any of the windows.

"It looks closed," I say.

"It is."

Nolan pulls into the parking lot and drives around to the back of the building. There is a single bright light mounted over a short flight of stairs leading down to a green metal door.

He stops across from the stairs and turns off the engine. "The coroner knows we're coming. He agreed to meet us when he called."

"He's dedicated."

Nolan looks at me. "How are you feeling?"

I repeat the question then look down at the bandage covering my missing finger. I want to answer him, but I can't. I feel nothing, no sadness, no anger, no fear.

Just emptiness.

Nolan waits, then says, "Let's get this over with."

– – –

My first steps are a struggle, but once I get my legs under me I feel pretty good. I follow Nolan across the parking lot to the stairs then down.

Nolan knocks on the green metal door. The sound echoes in the stairwell. He glances back at me on the steps and shakes his head.

"I told you not to open that goddamn bottle."

I tell him I'll make it, and I do.

We wait another minute, then Nolan knocks again. This time a bolt clicks and the door opens. The man standing inside is older, dark hair peppered with gray, and well over six feet tall. He's carrying a manila file in one hand and wearing a white lab coat that looks two sizes too small for his frame. The word *coroner* is stitched across the front pocket in heavy black thread.

He looks from Nolan to me, then back.

"Detective Nolan?"

Nolan nods, then introduces me and says, "We appreciate you sticking around tonight. I realize it's late."

The man mumbles something I don't quite hear, then stands aside and motions for us to come in. As we pass, I notice deep lines around his eyes and a smooth pink burn scar along the side of his jaw.

I start to ask him about it, but I change my mind.

It occurs to me that my focus is on everything except Diane and what I'm about to do. I went through too many group therapy sessions in detention not to know that this is a defense mechanism and that I'm trying to distance myself from what's coming.

This realization brings me back.

The coroner closes the door and slides the bolt, then walks past us down a long hallway.

We follow him.

The building is deserted. All the rooms are dark. The only light I see comes from one of the offices at the far end of the hall. The glow is soft and white and reflects silver off the polished tile floor.

Once inside the office, the coroner takes a set of keys from behind the desk. He looks at me, then opens the manila file he's carrying and reads, "Diane Reese, age twenty-seven. Husband, Jake Reese."

It's not a question.

He closes the file and says, "Is there anyone else we should notify? Any other family members?"

The air in the office feels thin and smells sharp, like ammonia. It doesn't mix well with the sour taste of alcohol in the back of my throat, and my head starts to spin. I can't think clearly.

"No, it's just the two of us."

"Okay." The coroner drops the file on the desk and says, "Follow me."

We walk back into the hall and head down, farther into the dark. There's no light, and all I see is the back of the coroner's white coat.

I try to stay focused.

A moment later I feel Nolan's hand on my arm, then hear him say, "You okay, Jake?"

"I'm fine," I say, and I almost believe it.

"All you have to do is look and say yes or no. A positive ID, that's it."

I tell him I know.

I tell him I've done this before.

The coroner stops in front of a large metal door and pulls back on the handle. He steps inside and flips a switch. A row of fluorescent lights flickers to life across the ceiling and turns the room a pale green.

There is a white autopsy table to the right, and six small doors built into the far wall.

For the first time since we arrived, I start to feel sick. I'd convinced myself, on some level, that this was all a mistake, that Diane wasn't really here, that she wasn't really dead.

Now I'm not sure.

The coroner crosses the room to the six doors along the far wall. I don't move.

Once again, I feel Nolan's hand on my arm, guiding me.

I pull my arm away and walk.

One step at a time.

The coroner waits. When I get close, he reaches down and pulls one of the handles. The door slides out like a drawer. There's a dull black body bag inside.

My lungs ache, and I realize I'm holding my breath.

The coroner looks at me and says, "Ready?"

I nod, don't speak, can't speak.

He unzips the top of the bag, then pulls away the sides and steps back.

When I look down, my breath comes out in a moan.

I can't hold it in anymore.

For a while, I just stare.

Behind me, the coroner says, "Can you confirm that this is the body of Diane Reese?"

I close my eyes. I can't find my voice.

All of my memories come racing back, one after another, too fast to hold on. All I can do is breathe.

I hear Nolan say, "Jake?"

Something inside me breaks, and I open my eyes.

They're both watching me.

The coroner asks me again if I can confirm that this is the body of Diane Reese.

This time I answer.

"Yes," I say. "It's her."

- 14 -

The coroner leads us back into the office. He takes a white binder off the shelf and starts flipping through pages. Nolan leans against the doorway, and I sit on a wooden chair in front of the desk.

The coroner reads the names of two funeral homes close to my house. "Do you have a preference?"

I shake my head. "It doesn't matter."

He writes one of the names on a piece of paper and tells me he'll have Diane's body transferred down in the next twenty-four hours. Then he says, "Have you decided on burial or cremation?"

"He doesn't have to do this now," Nolan says.

"No," the coroner says. "But state law requires a body be buried, embalmed, or cremated within seventy-two hours of death, so he needs to decide soon."

"Right," Nolan says. "But we can still give him some goddamn time before he—"

"Cremation," I say. "Diane wanted to be cremated."

The coroner nods and makes a note in the file. "I'll take care of it."

Nolan walks out into the hallway.

- - -

Before we can leave, the coroner lays out several papers for me to sign. I don't know what they are, and I don't ask. All I want is to go home.

I sign the papers.

The coroner takes a small envelope from his pocket and slides it to me across the desk. "Her personal items."

I pick it up and open the flap.

Diane's wedding ring is inside.

I feel my throat close. I swallow hard, then fold the envelope and slide it into my pocket.

I don't want to look at it, not here.

"Are we done?" I ask.

The coroner closes Diane's file and says, "We're done." Then he gets up and leads us out of the office and down the hall toward the metal door at the back of the building. "Detective, I'll have my report sent to you within the next forty-eight hours."

Nolan starts to say something, but the coroner ignores him and opens the back door. He stands to the side and waits for us to walk out. Nolan thanks him for meeting us so late.

The coroner nods and closes the door.

Nolan turns away and mumbles, "Nice fucking guy."

I pretend I didn't hear, then start up the steps to the parking lot.

When we get to the car, Nolan says, "Do you want me to drop you off at home, or is there someplace else you'd rather go?"

"Like where?"

"I don't know. I just thought you might want to be around friends tonight."

I tell him I want to go home.

We get in the car and drive back to the city in silence. This time, the bottle stays closed.

By the time we come out of the mountains, I've gone over the situation a dozen times in my head. I want to remember everything, starting with the night I was attacked and ending with see-ing Diane in the morgue.

The more I go over it, one thing seems clear.

Diane is dead because of me.

I don't want to believe it, but it's the truth and it sinks into me. I can't shake it. A few minutes later, another thought occurs to me, this one even worse.

"I could've stopped it."

Nolan looks at me. "What?"

"This is my fault, and I could've stopped it."

"There wasn't anything you could've done."

"When they sent my finger back in that package, I could've ended it right then, but I didn't."

Nolan hesitates. "I'm not following."

"One phone call and it would've been over. Diane would still be alive."

"You don't know that."

"Oh, yes I do."

Nolan is quiet for a moment, then he says, "I think you should stop before you say anything else."

"I'm just thinking out loud."

"Okay, but there are some things I can't pretend I didn't hear. Do you understand what I'm saying?"

I tell him I do, and for the rest of the trip neither of us says a word.

– – –

When we get to my house, Nolan pulls into the driveway. He reaches into his pocket and takes out his card and writes a num-ber on the back.

"My private cell phone." He holds the card out to me. "If you need to get in touch, call me directly."

I stare at the card, but I don't take it.

"Since when are you on my side?"

"There are no sides, Jake. I'm trying to help."

I almost laugh, but I manage to hold it back. "Sure." I take the card. "I'll call you."

He knows I'm lying, but I don't care.

From now on, I'm done with the police.

I get out and walk up the driveway to the front door. I watch Nolan pull away, then I turn and sit on the porch steps. I'm not ready to go inside, so for a while all I do is stare out at the dark street and listen to the dying October leaves rustle in the breeze.

Once I think I'm ready, I stand up and go inside. I don't turn on any lights, and I don't look around. Instead, I head straight for the kitchen and take a glass from the cabinet.

I open the Johnnie Walker bottle and pour.

When I finish the first, I pour another.

This time, I don't drink.

I stare at the clean, amber liquid and the light from above the stove reflecting off the surface. I can taste the first drink in the back of my throat, and something inside me clicks. I put the glass to my lips and finish it, then decide it'll be my last.

I've had enough.

I pick up the Johnnie Walker bottle and empty it into the sink. When I find the person behind everything that's happened, I want to meet him with a clear head.

No more running.

I drop the bottle in the trash, then grab the phone and walk down the hall to my office. My address book is in the top drawer of my desk. I search the pages until I find Gabby's number, then I sit down and dial.

It starts to ring.

I look up at the clock on the wall above my desk.

It's past midnight.

Late.

The phone keeps ringing.

I rest my elbows on the top of my desk and listen to the familiar voice in the back of my mind telling me this is a bad idea.

This time, it's easy to ignore.

The phone rings again. I wait for an answering machine to pick up, but it never does.

Hard to tell if I'm relieved or disappointed.

I hit the disconnect button, and the line goes dead.

I take it as a sign and decide to sleep on it before making this kind of decision. The idea of being able to sleep is ridiculous, but at least it sounds good.

I drop my address book back in the drawer, then shut off the light. I'm halfway to the kitchen when the phone rings. The sound echoes through the empty house.

My hand is shaking as I lift the receiver, but when I speak, my voice is steady.

The man on the other end asks, "Who is this?"

I close my eyes.

He was screening his calls.

Of course, he was screening his calls.

He asks again.

This time I answer. "It's Jake Reese."

Silence for a moment, then a short laugh.

"Well, what do you know," Gabby says. "I was starting to think you were dead."

PART II

- 15 -

My desk at work is covered with unread literary journals and ungraded student papers. I push them aside to clear space then take Lisa's card from my pocket and pick up the phone.

I dial the number and wait.

Outside, the sun is cold and bright. I can hear the sharp twitter of students passing below my window. Their voices blend together then fade away.

After the fifth ring, the line clicks and the answering machine picks up, again.

"This is Jake Reese. I'm trying to get in touch with Lisa Bishop."

I leave my number, then hang up and lean back in my chair. Diane's ring is sitting on my desk. I pick it up and turn it over in my hands, then set it on the desktop and spin it like a coin.

The sunlight shatters off the surface.

"Jake?"

I look up. Doug is standing in the doorway.

"Got a minute?"

I pick up Diane's ring and squeeze it in my hand, feeling it dig into my palm. "Come on in."

Doug steps inside and looks around. He points to a stack of books on one of the chairs and says, "Mind if I make some room?"

"Make yourself at home."

Doug moves the books to the floor, sits. "Who's Lisa Bishop?"

"What?"

"The phone call." He motions toward the doorway. "I overheard your message."

"Eavesdropping?"

"I wouldn't call it that, but now I'm curious. So, spill it. Who is she?"

"She's a psychic," I say. "In Arizona."

"You're kidding."

"I'm not."

Doug pauses. "Do I have to ask?"

I take Lisa's business card off my desk and hand it to him. "I found it in Diane's suitcase. I think she went to see her when she was down there last month. I want to know what they talked about."

Doug reads both sides of the card, frowns. "Why?"

I open my mouth, but I don't have an answer.

Talking to Lisa won't bring Diane back, and it won't change anything that's happened, so why do I want to talk to her? Why do I care?

"I want to know what she was thinking."

Doug nods. "How are you holding up?"

"Trying to keep busy."

"Is it helping?"

"If you came to talk about my feelings—"

"Just asking a question," Doug says. "You haven't said anything to anyone. It's been almost a week, and we're all in the dark. Is there going to be a funeral?"

"Haven't decided. When I'm ready to say something about it, I will."

"Okay." He hands me the card. "So, Lisa Bishop, the girl with the answers."

"What do you want me to do? I can't just sit around the house. I'll go crazy."

Doug motions to the stack of essays on my desk and says, "You could grade papers?"

"Lose myself in my work?"

"If it helps, sure." Doug leans forward and rests his elbows on his knees. "Speaking of work, there's something we need to discuss."

I watch him and wait.

"Anne Carlson came to see me. She told me she gave you a ride home the other night and that the police were at your house. Was that for Diane?"

I nod. "What did she want?"

"She was concerned. She said you didn't look good."

"But what did she want?"

"She asked me to come and talk to you," Doug says. "She wants my opinion on your mental state."

"My mental state?"

"That's how she put it."

"She wants to know if you think I'm crazy."

"She wants to know how you're holding up under the stress and if your personal life is getting in the way of your job."

"Is she going to fire me?"

"Of course not," Doug says. "She wants to help."

I stare at him and wait for him to go on.

Doug looks past me to the bookshelves behind my desk. "She mentioned a paid leave of absence until things settle down. It'll give you time to get back on your feet."

I let that sink in for a moment. "What did you tell her?"

"I told her I'd talk to you. She's worried about you. Everyone's worried."

I turn in my chair and face the window. "What do you think of the idea?"

"If you think the time off will help, take it. Get your life back in order. Start working on a new book. Do whatever you like, it's up to you."

"Can I think about it for a couple days?"

"It's a standing offer. Take your time and let me know what you decide."

"Thanks."

Doug slaps his knees with the palms of his hands, then pushes himself up and out of the chair. "Now that all that bullshit is out of the way, how about we go somewhere and get a drink and catch up? It's almost happy hour."

I shake my head. "Can't, I quit."

"Quit what?"

"Drinking," I say. "I'm done."

Doug watches me, trying to see if I'm joking. "That sounds rather drastic."

I shrug.

"We don't have to go back to The Body Shoppe if that's the problem. You can pick the spot this time."

"That's not it. I quit drinking."

"You're serious?"

I tell him I am.

"And what brought on this insanity?"

"It was time for a change," I say. "I can't afford to be clouded anymore. I have to stay focused."

"On what?"

"On what's coming."

Doug stares at me. "What exactly is coming?"

"I just can't afford to let my guard down, not right now." I pause. "I called Gabby."

"You did what?"

"It's fine. I explained the situation to him, and he offered to help."

"Help how?"

"He's going to find the two guys who attacked me."

"Jesus, Jake."

"I have to know who they are, and I want to talk to them, especially after what happened to Diane."

Doug shakes his head. "Diane was in a car accident."

I turn away, don't speak.

"Come on," Doug says. "Let's go out. I'll buy you a club soda, and we can talk about all of this."

"Not tonight." I point to the stacks of papers on my desk. "I've got essays to grade."

It was a joke, but Doug doesn't smile.

"Should I be worried about you, Jake?"

"No," I say. "I've got everything under control."

And like a fool, I believe it.

- 16 -

After the campus clears and the sun drops behind the mountains, I pack a couple stacks of ungraded papers into my bag then grab my keys and head home. When I get there, I go straight to the kitchen and check my voice mail.

There's a message, but it's not the one I was hoping to hear.

"Mr. Reese. This is Adam Fisher at Pearson's Funeral home. I'm calling to let you know we've received your wife's remains, and if you'd like to come by and select an urn, we can have them placed—"

I delete the message.

I stay at the table for a while, staring at nothing, trying not to think about Diane. I feel the tears pressing at the back of my eyes, and I fight to keep them there.

At first it works, then it doesn't.

I consider getting in my car and driving, no idea where, just away.

I don't want to be inside the house anymore. The rooms seem too big, too quiet, too full of ghosts.

I reach into my pocket and pull out Lisa's card. I think about the conversation I had with Doug in my office, how he'd asked why I wanted to talk to Lisa.

I didn't have an answer then, and I still don't.

Even if I did convince her to talk to me, what were the chances she'd tell me something I didn't already know? Diane was scared and confused and looking for answers.

Nothing new there.

It's more likely I'll make things worse. Lisa will hang up on me again, and I'll still be sitting in the kitchen, still bleeding for a drink, still wondering why my wife left and where she was going and what exactly happened to her on that empty road leading toward the desert.

But what if she doesn't hang up?

The possibility is all I need.

I pick up the phone and dial the number off the card.

The line rings, and I wait.

I tell myself I'm not going to leave another message. If the machine picks up, I'm going to hang up.

The line clicks. I wait for the familiar message asking me to leave my name and number, but it doesn't come.

This time, someone answers.

– – –

The woman on the other end of the line is all sunshine and smiles, until I tell her who I am.

"Mr. Reese, I don't want you to call here again."

"I need to know about Diane, and you're the only one who can help me."

"Out of the question," she says. "It's a matter of confidentiality, and I take it very seriously. Now please don't call here again—"

"Diane is dead."

Lisa stops talking, and for a while the only sound is the slow cycle of my breathing. The next time she speaks, her voice is soft, a whisper.

"She's dead?"

"Car accident," I say. "But I think she was killed."

Lisa makes a small choking sound in the back of her throat. "When?"

I start at the beginning with the attack in the parking lot, and I end with the car accident and driving up to Fairplay to identify her body.

Lisa listens, quiet, not hanging up.

When I finish I say, "I want to know if she said anything about us. I need to know if she was happy."

For a long time there's just silence, and then Lisa starts mumbling on the other end of the phone. I start to wonder if she heard me at all.

I ask her again.

This time she speaks.

She says, "That son of a bitch."

– – –

I stand in my kitchen with the phone pressed against my ear, saying the same thing over and over.

"What are you talking about?"

Lisa, still mumbling, isn't answering.

"Do you know what happened?"

She says she doesn't know anything, but it's a lie.

"I'm getting on the first flight I can find. I'm coming down to see you—"

This gets her attention.

"No!" Her voice is cold. "You're not."

"Then tell me what's going on."

"You can't come down here. If they—"

She stops.

I wait for her to go on, but she doesn't.

"Who is 'they'?"

"Mr. Reese, I can't help you. I just can't, and I'm sorry. Believe me."

"Don't do this," I say. "Tell me what happened to my wife. Did someone kill her?"

Lisa tells me she doesn't know anything, and even though I know it's a lie, I don't argue. She's not going to tell me, no matter how much I beg, at least not tonight.

It's time to cut my losses.

"Will you take my number and call me if you change your mind?"

"I have your number," she says. "Your messages."

I tell her it'll make me feel better if she writes it down. She hesitates, then agrees.

After she hangs up, I stay at the kitchen table for a while and try to figure out my next move. I know Lisa isn't going to call me back, so if I want to find out what she knows, I'll have to go to her.

She won't like it, but I don't care.

– – –

I find a flight leaving for Phoenix in the morning. I buy a ticket, then call and reserve a car. Sedona is a few hours' drive from the airport. If things go smoothly, I should be there by early afternoon.

Once the trip is booked, I grab my backpack from the closet and fill it with a change of clothes and a couple books to keep my mind busy on the plane. I look around for anything I might've forgotten, then zip the bag and slide it over my shoulder and turn out the light.

The phone rings.

My breath catches in my throat.

I carry the backpack to the kitchen and set it on the table. When I reach for the phone, the idea I might've been wrong about Lisa is right up front. She changed her mind and decided to talk to me after all.

Then I pick up the phone.

"Jake?"

It's not Lisa.

For a second, I can't find my voice. When I do speak, all I manage to say is, "Yeah?"

There's a pause, then the unmistakable scrape of a cigarette lighter and a long inhale.

I hear my heartbeat, and feel each second pass.

Gabby exhales smoke into the phone, and when he speaks, his voice sounds flat, tired.

He says, "We've got 'em."

- 17 -

At first, I'm not nervous, but that changes once I pull off the highway and cross under the Nineteenth Street viaduct into the warehouse district. I feel my pulse echoing in my head, and a dull ache building in the middle of my chest.

I remind myself that Gabby is a friend.

It helps a little.

There are no streetlights down here, and the buildings fade in and out of darkness as I drive. My instructions were to head west until I crossed the railroad tracks, then turn north and look for the sign.

He said it would be easy to find.

When I was a kid, Gabby owned a junkyard thirty miles outside the city. He had a homemade sign out front that said you could find anything you wanted inside, and he was probably right.

The yard seemed to go on forever.

I'd spend hours out there, wandering through a sea of crushed cars and mountains of rusted appliances. There were always new places to explore and treasures to find.

When I was a few years older, my father told me that besides being able to find whatever you wanted at Gabby's junkyard, you could also dispose of anything you wanted.

For a price.

"There are more bodies buried out there than over at Fairview Cemetery," he said. "One day, that place is going to be all over the news, you just watch."

He laughed when he told me, but I didn't.

There was nothing funny about Gabby.

Even as a kid, I knew something wasn't right about him, but my father didn't seem to notice. If he had one true friend in his life, it was Gabby, and he trusted him completely. So, when I was twelve and my dad went to prison for the first time, Gabby took me in.

I lived with him for four years before I found my own trouble and they sent me into juvenile detention.

Gabby would visit from time to time, and once he even told me he considered me a son. Now, driving through this deserted part of the city, all I can do is hope he still feels the same way.

I cross over the railroad tracks and turn right, heading north until I see a two-story brick building with a hand-painted sign out front.

Gabriel's Custom Wood Furniture.

Gabby was right. It was easy to find.

There's a heavy steel gate along the side of the building surrounding a large paved lot and loading dock. I drive by for a closer look, then pull into the parking lot across the street and shut off the engine.

It's quiet, and I can hear my heart beating against my ribs. I close my eyes for a moment, then open the door and step out. The wind sliding between the empty buildings is cold and smells like asphalt and oil.

I breathe it in deep and try to focus.

My feet don't want to move.

The two men who cut off my finger are inside, which means the answers I'm looking for are inside. I don't know if they're the ones who killed Diane, but I'm going to find out tonight, no matter what.

I stay by my car for a while and stare up at the grid of dark windows on the buildings lining the street. I try to shake the feeling I'm being watched, but it's hard.

Eventually, I cross the street to Gabby's place and walk up to the front door. There's a black button on the frame. I press it and hear a buzzer sound far away.

I hear a series of clicks from the locks, and then the door opens. The kid standing inside looks younger than my students. He is wearing a shoulder holster, and I see the handle of the gun by his armpit.

For a minute, we just stand there.

"What do you want?"

"I'm looking for Gabby."

He stares at me, doesn't move.

I look past him into the darkness. "Is he here or not?"

The kid's eyes go wide, just for a second, then he smiles. I know the smile. He's been assigned a job, and he thinks that makes him king. He knows he doesn't have to put up with anyone's shit.

I know this because ten years ago, that was me.

He opens his mouth to say something, but I interrupt and say, "No, don't talk. Just go find him."

The kid stops smiling. "Who the fuck are you?"

I start to tell him, and then I hear a door open somewhere behind him and a familiar voice say, "Hey, Jake."

The kid doesn't take his eyes off me, but the muscles in his face go loose. He waits until Gabby gets close, then he looks down and steps away from the door.

Gabby walks up with his arms out. He wraps them around me and pulls me in. For an instant, I feel my feet leave the floor. I can't help but smile.

When he lets go, he steps back and holds me at arm's length and says, "Holy shit, Jake."

It's the first time I've seen him in almost ten years, and I'm shocked at how little he's changed. His hair is a bit thinner, and the lines on his face are deeper, but the eyes, cold and blue, are exactly the same.

"It's good to see you," I say.

He nods. "Show me."

I hold up my left hand.

Gabby looks at the spot where my finger used to be, and something changes in his eyes. He grabs my hand and turns it over in his. I watch the jaw muscles twitch under his skin, and my heart starts to pound in my throat.

"Those two foreign fucks did this to you?"

I nod, don't speak.

"And your wife?"

"That's what I need to find out."

Gabby looks at me and smiles. "Don't worry about that, kid." He puts a hand behind my neck and squeezes. I try my best not to wince. "We'll find out. Count on it."

He lets go and motions for me to follow him.

"Come on in, I'll show you what I've been up to in my golden years." He slaps my chest. "You know I retired?"

"You retired?"

He holds up a hand, seesawing it back and forth. "I decided to give it a try after your old man went inside this last time. I thought it best to step out while I still had the legs to do it."

"I didn't know," I say. "I wouldn't have called."

"Bullshit. You're family, you and your dad." Gabby stops and turns to me. The lines on his face deepen. "I was real sorry to hear about what happened to him. He was a good man, you know that?"

I lie and tell him I do.

Gabby nods and leaves it at that, instantly forgotten.

"Well, come on in. I'll give you the nickel tour."

He turns and walks on, not looking back.

I step inside and let the door close behind me.

– 18 –

I follow Gabby down a short hall into an open room with high ceilings and metal shelves along the walls. The air smells sweet, like sawdust and wood stain, and the only light comes from a mounted security box in one corner.

Gabby steps past me and flicks a switch.

Several rows of lights flicker to life above us.

The room is filled with stacks of wood and half-built furniture. There are hand tools hanging on pegs along the wall, and reams of cloth and upholstery scattered across work benches.

"This is it," he says. "What do you think?"

"Impressive."

I follow him around the workshop while he points out all the different tools and the stacks of tables and chairs along the wall, some finished, some not.

"All this stuff is custom made. Good quality, too. It'll last, believe me."

"Looks like it."

"Got a couple kids working for me during the day. They're both younger than you. Musicians, I think, potheads, but good kids. Hard workers." He points to a door at the back of the shop and says, "That's my place."

"Your office?"

"My home."

"You live here? In the building?"

"Sure," he says. "It's not as quiet as the yard, but there's no traffic at night. After five o'clock, I'm the only living soul for two miles in any direction. It's like living in the country without the country."

"What about the yard? Did you sell it?"

Gabby shakes his head. "I'll never sell that place. I just wanted a change of scenery." He puts a hand on my shoulder. "You want to see where I live?"

– – –

We walk through the door in the back of the shop then up a steep flight of stairs to the second level. Gabby is telling me what the building looked like when he moved in, but all I can think about are the two guys who cut off my finger. They're here somewhere.

I do my best to be patient.

With Gabby, that's important.

When we get to the top of the stairs, Gabby opens the door and says, "This is it."

It's like stepping into Oz.

Hardwood floors, handwoven rugs, and full-length windows overlooking a jeweled city skyline. It is the opposite of what I'd been expecting, and for a moment, I don't know what to say.

Gabby smiles. "What do you think?"

I move toward the windows and look out at the wall of city lights and say, "It's amazing."

"It is, isn't it?" Gabby comes up next to me and puts his hands on his waist. "You get a little older, and you start appreciating the beautiful things in life."

"It is beautiful."

The two of us stare out the windows for a while, neither of us saying a word.

Then Gabby speaks.

"This place used to be a crematorium."

And all at once, I remember where I am.

I turn away from the window and look at Gabby.

"Got the old oven downstairs," he says. "The damn thing still works, too."

"Downstairs?"

"The basement. Here, take a look at this."

He leads me around the corner and points out a large arched metal door hanging on the wall.

"I popped it off the front of the oven and cleaned it with a pressure wash. It took forever, but once I polished her up, I thought she might look good on a wall."

"Like art."

"Exactly." Gabby grins, shows teeth. "Art."

I stare at the oven door, and I can't help but think he's right. It does look good. It's morbid and dark, but there's something fascinating about it, too.

Something almost beautiful.

– – –

Gabby finishes the tour on the roof.

He wants to show me his birds.

"Racing pigeons," he says. "It's a hobby, and a little side business of mine. Something to do in retirement."

I laugh under my breath.

"What's so funny?"

"You being retired. I can't picture it."

"Can't stay young forever, Jake. You might not see it, but things have changed out there. The world is different, and there's no place for guys like me anymore."

"What are you talking about?"

"The players are all different. Now it's the people in the suits who control everything. They talk and they negotiate and they make deals. They're the ones you have to worry about, not the guy running things from the back booth at the neighborhood bar."

"You were always more than that."

"Was I?" Gabby shakes his head. He reaches into his pocket and takes out a package of sunflower seeds and pours a few into his palm. "These days I've got my shop and I've got my birds. That's enough for me. The rest doesn't matter anymore."

I watch Gabby open the cage and lay the seeds across a long wooden feed tray. I think about what he said, and as I watch him, I have a hard time not believing him.

He looks happy.

I think back over all the time I spent with him as a kid, and I can't remember ever seeing him smile.

I wait until he closes the cage. Then I motion to the birds and ask, "What kind of business is this?"

"A small one," he says. "I'll rent the white ones out for weddings. Some people like to release birds, and you wouldn't believe how much they're willing to pay to do it."

"I thought you released doves at weddings."

"Doves don't have the homing instinct. You release doves and all you're doing is feeding the hawks." He taps the wire on one of the cages and the birds shuffle inside. "These guys here, they're smart. They know what's out there, and they always find their way home when things turn bad."

He looks at me, and something passes between us.

Neither of us says a word.

Gabby turns back to the cage and starts making soft clicking noises at the birds.

I look out at the city lights and wait.

"The little one doesn't have a tongue," Gabby says. "Someone cut it out."

At first I think he's talking about the birds.

But he's not.

"The big one had some fight in him when we brought him here, so I split one of his fingertips down the middle with a wood chisel and pried the bone apart with a shim. That settled him down."

The inside of my mouth turns sour.

I swallow hard.

"I haven't said a word to either of them, so they're scared. I wanted to let you ask the questions. Are you okay with that?"

I tell him I am.

"Good, because he's ready to talk."

"Are you sure?"

"Of course I'm sure."

"What if he doesn't?"

Gabby turns back to the birds. He takes a deep breath, holds it, then says, "I'm not going to kill anyone, kid. That's where I draw the line these days."

I'm not sure whether to believe him or not, so I do the smart thing and keep my mouth shut.

Gabby looks at me and smiles. "Don't worry about it, he'll talk. And if he doesn't..." He holds up his hand and wiggles his fingers. "I've got a lot of shims."

- 19 -

I follow Gabby downstairs and through the workshop to the cement loading dock behind the building. There is a man in a heavy black coat sitting on a folding chair next to a split metal door. When he sees Gabby, he stands and presses a call button on the wall.

A few seconds later, I hear a motor, far away.

When it stops, the man pulls a canvas strap on the door, and the two sides split apart, opening onto a freight elevator.

"We don't go down together," Gabby says. "They only see me when it's necessary." He taps the side of his head with one finger. "Fuck with their minds a bit."

I stare at the man in the black coat standing outside the elevator. "Are you sure you retired?"

Gabby laughs, and once again the sound surprises me.

"That's Kevin. He'll take you inside and bring you back up when you're ready."

I nod.

"You okay with this, Jake?"

"I'm fine."

"Because if you're not, I can step in and—"

"I said I'm fine."

Gabby watches me for a minute, silent.

"Just anxious," I say. "Too many things in my head. I can't keep them straight."

Gabby stands in front of me and puts a hand on my shoulder. "The only thing you need to think about is your wife."

The words are like an electric shock, and all my doubts over what I'm about to do burn away.

"Don't lose your focus. Don't forget why you're here." He pats my cheek, once, hard. "We'll talk when you come up."

I feel like I should say something, but there's nothing else to say. It's time.

Gabby looks past me and nods toward Kevin, then he turns and walks back into the workshop.

— — —

I step into the elevator, and Kevin slides the doors shut. There is only one button on the keypad. He presses it, then steps back and leans against the wall.

Nothing happens.

I say, "We're not moving."

"Give it a minute." He points to a black camera lens above the door. "They can be slow."

I look up at the camera. "Someone's watching us?"

"The elevator is controlled from the basement, unless you have a key. They like to see who is coming." He nods toward the lens. "Go ahead, smile."

I don't smile.

"How long have you worked for Gabby?"

"Three years," he says. "Came here on a bus from Iowa. I figured this place couldn't be any worse."

"Were you right?"

"Hell yes. Iowa, are you kidding? Even when he had me out at the yard, it was better than Iowa."

"You're not out at the yard anymore."

"Nope, not anymore."

I watch him, trying to guess his age. He looks young, probably under twenty, and I'm not surprised. Gabby has always recruited street kids. He takes them in and gives them a job and a place to stay, but more than that, he gives them a place to belong. He gives them a family.

A lot of them don't stick around for long, but the ones who do are loyal forever, and Gabby knows it.

Sometimes I wonder if I was any different.

"What about you?" Kevin asks.

"What about me?"

"How long have you known the old man?"

"The old man?"

Kevin clears his throat and stands a bit straighter. "Mr. Meyers. How long have you known Mr. Meyers?"

"Gabby," I say. "I've known him all my life."

He nods. "I guess that explains it."

"Explains what?"

"What he did down here." Kevin pauses. "He made this one personal. I've never seen anything like it."

I stare at him for a moment, silent, then the elevator starts to move and I look away.

We go down, slow.

All at once, my legs feel weak.

I lean back against the elevator wall and look down at the streaks of dried paint on the floor. There's a tiny voice inside my head, screaming at me, telling me this is a mistake and to go back up and get in my car and go home. It tells me to forget all about this place and to rebuild my life before it's too late.

But I know it's already too late.

Kevin doesn't say anything else, and I'm glad. I don't want to talk anymore.

Instead, I listen to the hum of the motor and feel myself fall.

- - -

There are two men waiting outside the elevator when it stops, both wearing handguns in shoulder holsters. Neither of them says a word when Kevin slides the door open and we step out.

The basement is large and filled with furniture and cardboard packing crates. There is a desk in the corner with a monitor showing the inside of the elevator.

The air feels heavy and wet.

I look around. "Where are they?"

Kevin walks to the desk and grabs a key ring off the monitor. He motions for me to follow and leads me around a stack of shipping pallets to a long metal door. He unlocks the door and pushes it to the side. The door opens, scratching along a rusted track in the ceiling.

I step closer, and the smell hits me in waves, warm and ripe, each one stronger than the last.

Blood, vomit, and piss.

I cough and put a hand to my mouth.

Kevin watches, but he doesn't say a word.

I clear my throat and move toward the open door. The smell gets stronger with each step, but this time I'm prepared.

The room is dark except for two beams of light shining down from a pair of industrial-sized security lamps mounted in the ceiling. The beams spotlight a man sitting at a table in the middle of the room. Everything else is in shadow.

The man at the table is sitting with his back to the door, his head hanging limp to one side. I move closer and notice the thick leather straps around his shoulders and arms, pinning him to the chair.

There is a pool of blood on the floor under him. It runs in long streams toward a sunken drain a few feet away. Just past the drain, I can see the shadow of the crematory oven, dark and open.

I try not to look at it.

"Is he awake?" I ask.

"He can be."

The air in the room is hot, and I feel a slow line of sweat run down the center of my back. I shift my weight from one foot to the other, afraid to stop moving. Then I start toward the man at the table.

Halfway there, I notice the little one sitting in the corner with his arms stretched over his head. His wrists are bound tight with wire and held up by a link chain that disappears into the shadows above him. The left side of his face is broken. His eye is swollen shut.

I stare at him for a moment before I realize his other eye is open, and he's watching me.

Seeing him changes something inside me.

I feel steady again, ready to work.

I look over at Kevin, standing in the doorway.

He nods, then steps back and closes the door.

- 20 -

I walk around to the front of the table.

The big guy's hand is strapped, palm down, to a thick block of wood that makes me think of a cutting board. His fingers are spread wide and pinned in place by five heavy industrial staples just below his knuckles.

There is blood everywhere.

At first I think Gabby must've split the guy's hand in two, but he didn't. He did exactly what he'd said.

The man's middle fingertip is forked in the center, and there is a wooden shim wedging the bone apart, almost to the breaking point.

Even though Gabby told me what to expect, seeing it makes my stomach twist and my mouth fill with water.

I look away and think about Diane.

The more I picture her in my mind, the less any of this bothers me.

I step closer and stare at the man's face. He doesn't look as bad as the other one, but he doesn't look good. His nose is broken, his eyes are closed, and the front of his shirt is covered in blood and dried vomit.

I lean in. "Wake up."

The man doesn't move.

I tap the side his face, soft.

His eyes flutter open, distant and unfocused.

I wait.

Eventually, he lifts his head and looks around. It takes a minute before he realizes where he is, and then his lips start to shake.

"What do you want?"

I can't tell if it's the accent or damage from the beating, but the words rumble out and blend together, making it hard to understand.

"Do you remember me?"

He turns his head back and forth, scanning as much of the room as possible, ignoring me. I ask him again, and this time when he doesn't answer, I press my thumb against the shim embedded in his finger.

This gets his attention.

When he calms down, I ask him again.

The man shakes his head. "I don't know you."

I show him my left hand with the missing finger, and something changes in his eyes.

"No, no, no," he says. "Please."

"Who are you?"

"It was just a job," he says. "We didn't want to hurt anyone, not bad, I swear—"

"A job?"

He nods. "Just a job."

"Who hired you?"

He mumbles something. I lean in close, and he flinches, closes his eyes.

"I want a name. Tell me who hired you."

He starts mumbling again, and the next time I speak, I have to force myself to keep my voice calm.

"The man who brought you here," I say. "The one who did this to your hand? He's waiting outside."

I hear the man's breath catch in his throat.

"He wants to see if you'll tell me what I want to know. If you do, you go home. If you don't, then he comes back in here."

The big guy whimpers, says, "I'm just a baker."

I ignore him. "I can't tell you what he'll do, because he's capable of absolutely anything."

The man shakes his head. There are tears now.

I reach down and touch the shim. He twitches and makes a high whining sound in the base of his throat.

"Tell me who hired you."

"We wanted to open a bakery, we didn't mean—"

"Who is we?"

"My brother," he says. "We came here, we had to leave, they would've killed him if we stayed."

"Leave where?"

"St. Petersburg. They hung him in the street, in front of our mother. They left him to die."

I look past him to the man in the corner.

He looks back, unafraid.

"Someone hired you to cut off my finger?"

"Yes."

"Why?"

"I don't know." He coughs, and blood sprays across the table. "We were told where you'd be and what we were supposed to do. He was very specific."

The man looks down and starts whispering to himself about starting over, about not living this kind of life. As he talks, a long trail of blood and saliva runs out of his mouth onto his shirt.

I bend down and say, "I want a name."

The man shakes his head.

"You give me a name and you and your brother can go. But this is the last time I'm going to ask. If you don't tell me, I'm going to leave, and then my friend—"

"No, please."

"—will come back."

"I only saw him one time."

"Last chance."

"He was a cop."

I stop talking.

"He told us we'd be deported and sent home unless we agreed to help." He looks at me, his eyes pleading. "We can't go back. They'll kill us both."

"Who was he?"

"He gave us money. It was just a job, I swear."

"What was his name?"

"I only saw him once."

I reach for his hand, fast. He jerks back in the chair and screams.

"Give me a goddamn name!"

"I don't—" He hesitates. "Nolan. Dan Nolan."

I don't say anything right away. I can't. My throat closes, and the floor under me seems too far away.

I bend down, eye level, and ask him to tell me again.

"His name was Nolan. I swear on the mother of Christ that's all I know. Please."

The air tastes stale in my throat.

"I want you to be sure."

"I don't know anything else, I don't."

"The name, are you sure about the name?"

The man nods.

"You saw a badge? He was a detective?"

"Yes, I think, I don't know. Please, you said we could go."

I push myself to my feet and follow the line of blood toward the drain. There are no thoughts in my head, just questions and rage.

"Did he hire you to kill my wife?"

The man looks at me, and I see the confusion on his face. "No." He shakes his head. "Your finger, that's all."

Every muscle in my body aches. I don't want to be down here anymore, and I don't want to hear anything else. But I have to be sure.

I walk back to the table and press hard on the shim.

The man doesn't scream this time, but he feels it.

"Was it you?" I ask. "Did Nolan—"

"I don't—"

"Did you kill her?"

"No," he says. "I killed no one."

He keeps giving me the same answer, and I keep working the shim back and forth until I'm sure he's telling me the truth. Then I grab both sides and tear it out.

He screams.

I turn the bloody shim over in my hand, then set it on the table in front of him and say, "Nothing personal, okay?"

The man looks at the shim, then up at me.

His eyes are distant, tired.

A moment later he drops his head, his shoulders shake, and he begins to cry.

- 21 -

Gabby motions toward the hallway. "Second door down. The light switch is by the mirror."

I follow his directions, focusing on each step.

When I get to the bathroom, I turn on the light, then lock the door behind me. My head is spinning. I lean over the sink and wait for it to pass. Once it does, I run my hands under the water and start to wash away the blood.

I try to stay calm and plan my next move, but I can feel every muscle in my body straining, ready to snap. My breath is heavy, and I realize I'm rocking back and forth, shifting my weight from one foot to the other.

I can't think clearly.

Every time I close my eyes, all I see is Nolan in my house the day I found my finger in the mail. I remember the way he looked at me and the accusing tone in his voice. It burns inside me.

My mind wanders.

I start thinking about the .38 I keep in my closet at home, how I can go back and grab it tonight. I could call Nolan's cell number and tell him to meet me.

Then I could ask my own questions.

I turn the water to cold then wash my face and run my hands through my hair. When I look up, I lean against the sink and stare at myself in the mirror.

I don't like what I see.

I know what I'm considering is crazy, but I can't stop thinking about Nolan. I have to know the truth, and I have to hear it from him, no matter what it takes.

My thoughts keep going back to the gun.

I never told Diane about it. She made it clear she never wanted one in the house. I'd never lived anywhere without a gun, but she didn't care.

So, it became my secret.

Old habits.

Someone knocks. I hear Gabby's voice, muted through the door. "You okay in there, Jake?"

I open the door. Gabby looks at me, then past me toward the blood in the sink.

"I'll clean it."

He points over his shoulder. "Come on out so we can talk. You can take care of that later."

"Give me a minute?"

Gabby taps his watch. "Clock's ticking, Jake. Make it fast."

– – –

Gabby is at the top of the stairs talking to Kevin.

I sit on the couch and wait.

There is a white ceramic dove on the coffee table. It looks cheap, like something you'd buy off the television in the middle of the night, but when I pick it up there's weight to it. I turn it over in my hands and trace the long curved outline of the wings with my finger.

Behind me, I hear the door close and Kevin's footsteps trail off down the stairs.

Gabby takes a pack of cigarettes off one of the bookshelves and sits across from me on a worn leather chair. He taps a cigarette out of the pack and uses it to point at the ceramic dove in my hand.

"Your dad gave me that before he died."

"Is that right?" I set it back on the table.

"It's yours if you want it," Gabby says. "I'm sure he would've wanted you to have it anyway."

I almost laugh.

Gabby lights his cigarette. "Kevin's taking those two over to Central Hospital. He'll drop them out front. They should be fine."

"We're done with them?"

"Didn't you get what you wanted?"

I don't say anything.

Gabby watches me. "Tell me about this cop," he says. "What do you know about him?"

"He's the detective assigned to my case. He took me to ID Diane's body."

"He took you?"

I go over the details of the drive to Fairplay and our meeting with the coroner. As I talk, the look on Gabby's face changes.

"What's wrong?"

"That doesn't sound right."

"It's what happened."

Gabby gets up and grabs an ashtray off one of the bookshelves. He taps his cigarette over it as he sits back on the chair.

"I've never heard of a coroner doing anything like that. Those guys are meticulous. They do everything by the book."

"What are you saying?"

Gabby shrugs the question away, but I don't give up.

I ask again.

"It's strange, that's all." He opens his mouth to say something else, hesitates, then says, "Do you think this cop had something to do with your wife's death?"

"I don't know, but I'm going to find out."

"How?"

I think about my .38 at home, but I keep that to myself. I know exactly how Gabby would respond. "I haven't figured that out yet."

Gabby watches, trying to see if I'm lying.

After a while, the quiet gets to be too much and I say, "What would you do if you were me?"

"That doesn't matter," he says. "All that matters is what you're *not* going to do."

"What's that?"

"You're not going to do anything stupid."

I laugh.

"Something funny?"

"Diane told me the same thing when I talked to her about calling you."

"Maybe she was right." Gabby crushes his cigarette in the ashtray, then sets it on the coffee table next to the ceramic dove. "You've got a flight booked for Phoenix in the morning, don't you?"

"I do."

"Good. I'll make a couple calls while you're gone, see what we can find out about this cop."

"I'm not going to Phoenix. Not now."

Gabby ignores me. "When you get back, I'll know more about the situation. We can go from there."

I tell him again, "I'm not going to Phoenix."

Gabby eases back in his chair and brushes his hand over his knee and says, "Why not?"

"Because Nolan is here."

"He'll still be here when you get back."

I start to argue, but Gabby holds up his hand, stopping me. "What do you think you're going to do? Pull a cop off the street? You're smarter than that, Jake."

"I have to do something."

"Not that," Gabby says. "And not with my help. I won't go after a cop."

"You've done it before."

There's a flash of anger in Gabby's eyes, enough to turn everything inside me cold.

"That was a long time ago," he says. "Things were different back then. I was different."

We're both quiet for a while, and then Gabby leans forward. "We can't rush this one. All I'm asking is for you to be patient. Give me a couple days to check it out, lay the groundwork, find out who's involved."

"We know who's involved."

"No, we don't," Gabby says. "I don't think this cop is the one we're after."

I point to the door leading downstairs and say, "If you think he lied to me, why are you letting them go?"

"Nolan might've hired them, but someone else hired Nolan. That's how these cops work, unless he had a personal reason to come after you."

"He didn't."

"Then that means someone else is out there pulling the strings. Someone else hired Nolan."

"So, we find Nolan and ask him."

Gabby looks down at the floor then rubs the sides of his head with his fingertips and says, "Do you know why I've never been to prison?"

I shake my head.

"Because I'm patient. I never make a move without thinking it through and waiting for the exact right time." He looks up at me. "You, on the other hand, are not patient. You're impulsive, just like your dad, and that makes you dangerous."

"I'll be fine."

"I'm thinking about me," he says. "Your head is a mess, and that makes you someone I don't need around, especially since we're dealing with cops."

"I'm not going to walk away. I can't."

"I don't want you here, Jake." There's an edge to Gabby's voice. "If you want my help, you'll go to Phoenix and clear your fucking head."

I don't push.

I know better.

Gabby watches me for a while, then reaches for the pack of cigarettes. "Why don't you head home and get some rest? Tomorrow, get on that plane. Find out whatever it is you want to find out, and I'll take care of things here."

I don't like it, but the decision's been made.

We get up and walk to the door.

Gabby stops at the top of the stairs and tells me to call him when I get to Phoenix. "I want a number where I can reach you if I need to."

"It's killing me to walk away like this."

"You're not walking away."

"Diane's dead, and all the answers I need are right here. If I'm not walking away, then what the hell am I doing?"

Gabby pauses, says, "You're saying good-bye to your wife."

- 22 -

I pull out of the parking lot and head west toward the highway. There's no traffic tonight, and as I turn onto the on-ramp and pick up speed, I don't want to stop.

I feel like I could drive forever.

I think of Diane and wonder if she felt the same way before she died. Was she really on her way to Phoenix, or was she just driving to clear her mind?

It doesn't take long before my thoughts turn bad, and I do my best to push them away.

It's not time to think about her.

Not yet.

Instead, I go over everything that I learned tonight and try to make sense of it all. Why would Nolan hire those two men to attack me? And was Gabby right? Was someone else pulling the strings?

If there was, then why didn't they just get it over with? Why toy with me without telling me who they are or what they want?

And what about Diane?

Why kill her?

Something Nolan said while we were driving into the mountains comes back to me, and it doesn't go away. He said it wasn't my fault, not this time.

Did he know something?

If he'd been behind the attack in the parking lot, could he also have been involved in Diane's murder? Was that why he was the one who took me to ID her body in the middle of the night?

My memories of that night are broken, clouded by the alcohol. Still, drunk or not, nothing about that night makes sense. It didn't then, and it doesn't now.

Gabby was right.

That's not the way things are done.

The more I think about it, the more it burns at me. I'm convinced something is there. All I have to do is put it together.

I look at the clock on the dashboard. It's not as late as it feels, and I start to think about Nolan.

I can find him tonight.

I can make him tell me the truth.

It's a bad idea, but it's all I can think about.

– – –

I park in my driveway and walk up to the front door. The porch light is off, and it takes a minute for me to get my key in the lock. Once I do, I open the door and go inside.

The house is dark except for a pale yellow glow coming from the stove in the kitchen. Keeping a light on had been Diane's idea. She hated coming home to a dark house. It was her habit. Now it's mine.

I walk down the hall to my office and dig through the papers on my desk. I'm looking for the card Nolan gave me the night he took me to ID Diane's body, but I don't see it. I check the drawers and the bookshelves, then turn and walk back out to the living room.

The card is sitting on the coffee table.

I pick it up and flip it over. His cell number is written on the back. I stare at it for a moment and try to decide on my next move. Nolan is my only chance to find the answers I need, and I don't want to play my hand over the phone. In person, I can make him cooperate.

I take Nolan's card back to my office. I drop it on the desk, then turn and run my hand along the top of the bookshelf until my fingers touch a set of keys on a small silver ring. I flip through them until I find the right one, then I unlock the bottom drawer of my desk.

My .38 is inside.

I feel an old twinge of guilt knowing I kept the gun even though Diane didn't want it in the house. I used to get around feeling bad by telling myself I only had it for emergencies. I'm not sure if this is an emergency, but I know I'll have a better chance getting Nolan to answer my questions with the gun than without it.

I take the gun and a loaded clip and carry them back to the kitchen. I slide the clip into the gun, check the safety, then set it on the counter and pick up the phone.

I dial Nolan's cell number off the card, pausing a second before hitting the last digit. I think about Gabby's advice to wait and let him see what he can find out, but I don't want to wait. All I've done is wait.

I want answers, and I want them now.

I dial the last number then put the receiver to my ear and wait for it to ring.

There's movement behind me, then a voice.

"Jake."

I turn and something slams against my face.

I feel my nose go, and the world explodes in light. I drop to my hands and knees. Blood pools on the tile floor under me. The phone hits the ground. For a second, I think I hear it ringing, and then I realize the sound is coming from the man standing over me.

From his cell phone.

The man picks up my phone and presses the disconnect button. His cell phone stops ringing.

"Nolan?"

My voice is broken. When I look up, blood runs down the back of my throat and I start to cough.

The floor shifts under me.

Nolan puts the phone back in the cradle, then grabs my hands and pulls them behind my back. There is the familiar click of handcuffs, and then I'm up. He leads me through the kitchen and out the back door. We cross the yard to the wooden gate leading into the alley.

Nolan's cruiser is parked behind my house.

"What are you doing?"

He doesn't answer. Instead, he pops the latch on the trunk and pushes me inside.

I'm lying on my back, looking up at him.

"What the hell are—"

Nolan leans forward and punches me hard in the stomach, and all the air rushes out of my lungs.

"Don't fucking talk," he says. "Just keep your mouth shut, do you understand?"

I can't breathe, so I don't speak.

The blood from my nose is running across my cheeks and down my throat. I feel like I'm drowning, and it takes all I've got not to panic.

Nolan slams the trunk shut, and I'm in darkness.

I listen for his footsteps, but all I hear is my own rapid, wet breathing. A few seconds later, the car dips and the driver's side door slams shut. The engine starts and I feel the exhaust settle in my lungs.

I can't smell it, but I know it's there.

Once we're moving, I roll to my side and cough some of the blood out of my throat. My sinuses feel like they've been packed tight with gasoline-soaked cotton and set on fire. Breathing through my nose is out of the question.

All I can do is close my eyes and listen to the low buzz of the road passing beneath the tires, and wait.

At least I found Nolan.

And one way or another, it'll all be over soon.

- 23 -

We drive for a long time.

At first I try to follow the turns so I know where we're going, but it doesn't take long before I lose track and I'm lost. When we finally stop, everything is quiet except for the wind and the occasional car passing somewhere far away.

I hear the driver's side door open, then Nolan's footsteps on loose gravel. They're close at first, then they move away and I can't hear them anymore.

The handcuffs are cutting into my wrists, and my fingers are numb. I shift my weight to take some pressure off my hands, but all I do is make it worse.

I don't know how much time has passed before Nolan's footsteps come back. They stop next to the car, and I hear a delicate chime of keys. He unlocks the latch and opens the trunk.

I look up at Nolan standing over me.

It's dark, and behind him a canopy of oak trees sway in the wind. He's frowning.

"How you feeling?"

There's a hint of an apology in his voice.

Just a hint.

"Let me out," I say.

Nolan looks around then reaches in and grabs my arm and pulls me up. I ease my legs over the side, but when I try to stand, everything spins around me. I sit on the edge of the trunk until it stops.

Once I feel steady, I try again.

At first I don't know where I am, and then I see the marble columns of the park pavilion to my left and the high-rise apartments towering over the trees to the north.

Memorial Park.

"What the hell are we doing here?"

Nolan doesn't answer.

He takes my arm and walks me around the car to the passenger side and leans me against the door, then goes back to the trunk and pulls out a small black tackle box. He opens it on the ground and says, "I've got a saline wash and some gauze we can use to get that blood off."

"It won't help. My nose is broken."

"Maybe not."

There is no maybe. I've had my nose broken before, and I know how it feels. It's not something you forget. I start to explain this to him, then I decide it really doesn't matter and stop talking.

I turn and look around the parking lot. There are no other cars, just a scatter of trees and shadows stretching across the empty lawn.

In the moonlight, everything is blue.

The idea of running crosses my mind, but I don't know why. I don't want to get away, I want answers, and Nolan is the only person who can give them to me.

It's not how I planned it, but it's what I wanted.

"Are you going to explain any of this?" I try to sound tough, but with my nose smashed flat against my face, my voice comes out thin and weak. "Why did you bring me here?"

"Because I was asked to."

"By who?"

"I think it's best if you don't talk."

"Why?"

Nolan shakes his head, doesn't look up.

"Why are we out here?" I ask.

Nolan closes the tackle box. He stands in front of me and stares at my nose for a moment, then uncaps the bottle of saline. "Just be thankful I was the one who came for you. Things could've been a lot worse."

"You mean I could've lost another finger?"

Nolan ignores me and pours the saline onto a folded strip of gauze. "Keep still."

I do the best I can, but he makes it tough.

"All I know is you fucked up," he says. "You must've really pissed someone off."

"Who?"

"How the hell would I know?"

"You're working for them."

Nolan presses the gauze hard against my cheek and I wince. "No," he says. "I'm not. I don't know any more than you do."

I keep quiet until he finishes wiping the blood off my face, then say, "Did you kill Diane?"

"What?"

"My wife. Did you kill her, or did you hire someone to do that for you, too?"

Nolan punches me in the stomach, hard.

I bend forward and try not to throw up.

For a long time, I can't breathe.

Nolan stands over me, watching. "I've never killed anyone, do you understand?" He pauses. "I'm not like you fucking people."

When I can, I say, "I know you hired the men who cut off my finger. I talked to them, they told me everything."

Nolan steps closer. I get ready for him to hit me again, but he doesn't. Instead, he says, "What are you talking about?"

I tell him what happened at Gabby's place, leaving out the names and a lot of the detail. Whatever Nolan's plans are, I don't think they include arresting me. Still, I've learned not to take chances with cops.

When I finish talking, Nolan walks back to the tackle box on the ground behind the car. He opens the lid and drops the bloody gauze inside.

"They told me you threatened to have them deported if they didn't do what you asked," I say. "Is that true?"

"Deported?"

"Is it true?"

Nolan puts the tackle box back in the trunk and slams it shut. He stands for a while, not moving, then leans against the car with his head down.

"All this happened tonight?" he asks.

"Just a couple hours ago."

"What else did they say? I want to know all of it."

"Why?"

"Because it might be important."

There's something in his voice that stops me from arguing. I start at the beginning, and I go over every detail of the conversation I had with the man in Gabby's basement.

This time I leave nothing out.

Nolan listens, and when I finish he says, "He told you they were bakers?"

"Was he lying?"

"I don't know. How many bakers have you met who've had their tongues cut out of their mouths?"

I don't answer him, and for a while neither of us says a word.

"Did he tell you this story before or after your friend did that to his hand?"

"After."

"And how bad was it?"

I think about the blood covering the table and pooling around the chair, the way it snaked across the floor toward the sunken drain in the middle of the room.

"Bad."

"And this friend of yours just let them go?"

"He had them dropped off outside the hospital."

Nolan looks away. "Christ."

I keep quiet and let the pieces fall into place.

"You didn't hire them, did you."

"I didn't even know they existed until I questioned you about the attack."

I watch him and try to see if he's lying.

He sees what I'm doing, and he frowns. "I said I didn't hire them."

"Then who are they?"

Nolan shakes his head. "I really don't know."

- 24 -

"Someone contacted me the day your case landed on my desk," Nolan says. "It was just after I came to your house that first time. Do you remember?"

"Of course I do."

"When I got back to my office, I found a manila envelope with my name on it. There were things inside—" Nolan pauses, then comes around the car to where I'm standing. "That night they called and told me to bury your case."

"Who's they?"

"I didn't ask."

"Someone calls and tells you to cover up an investigation and you do it, just like that?"

"You're not the only one with a past, Jake." He takes a crumpled pack of cigarettes from his pocket and puts one in his mouth. "They were persuasive."

"They blackmailed you?"

Nolan lights his cigarette. "I've done some things I'm not proud of, things I've put behind me."

"Things they know about?"

"That's right," he says. "All I want to do is keep my badge. Do you understand?"

I tell him I do, and it's the truth.

I just don't care.

"You have no idea who they are?"

"No, and even if I did I wouldn't tell you."

"Why not?"

Nolan smiles. "What kind of people do you think we're dealing with here?"

I don't answer.

"You had a man look you in the eye tonight and convince you that he was someone else. And he did it after your friend had worked him over. Can you imagine that kind of control?"

"How do you know he was lying?"

"He had to be," Nolan says. "It was an act, the pain, the fear, all of it."

"That's not possible."

"I'm afraid it is." Nolan looks down at his cigarette and rolls it back and forth between his fingers. "Those are the kind of people we're dealing with."

"I don't believe it," I say. "You weren't there. You didn't see what I saw in that basement."

"What did you see? Tell me."

I start to go over it again. I tell him about the air in the room, hot and thick and heavy with the smell of blood and piss. I tell him about seeing the two of them lumped on either side of the basement. The big one strapped to the table, and the little one...

I stop talking.

The little one.

I picture him in my mind, sitting in the corner, his hands tied with wire and stretched over his head, blood running down his arms. I can still see his face, broken and bruised, one eye swollen shut, the other wide open and fearless, watching me.

Why wasn't he scared?

My chest aches, and I can't find the words.

I look at Nolan, and he sees it in my face. He smiles and drops his cigarette on the ground at his feet. "It is what it is."

"But it doesn't make sense," I say. "If it's true, then why are you here? Why are you involved?"

"I told you." He motions toward my finger. "They wanted to make sure no one investigated the attack. It's the reason I kept looking at you instead of finding—"

"No, why are you out here tonight? Someone told you to bring me here. Why would they do that?"

Nolan doesn't speak.

I keep talking.

"If you're right about all this, then why would they need you to come to my house and get me? If they wanted me, they could've grabbed me that night in the parking lot, or any other night. Why did they have you bring me here tonight?"

Nolan shakes his head, silent.

"It sounds like they wanted us both here."

Right away, something changes in Nolan's eyes. He steps back from the car and looks at his watch, then out toward the entrance to the park. I start to say something else, but he holds up a hand, stopping me.

"No more talking."

I tell him that's fine with me.

My broken nose is throbbing and sending waves of pain through the center of my skull. It hurts to breathe, and talking is worse.

I lean back against the car and adjust my wrists so the handcuffs don't cut off the circulation. I hear the wind passing through the trees, and I try to focus on the sound, reminding myself why I'm here.

I close my eyes and think about Diane.

It makes everything all right.

When I open my eyes again, Nolan is gone.

– – –

The wind picks up and turns cold.

I pace back and fourth to keep the blood flowing. I can't feel anything below my elbows, and every step I take sends jagged flashes of pain through my head.

I inch myself down to the ground and use the car as a shield. It helps, but not much.

A few minutes pass, and then I hear footsteps on the gravel.

I try to stand, but with my hands cuffed I can't get my legs under me, so I stay where I am and I wait.

The footsteps get closer. Nolan comes around the side of the car. He sees me on the ground, and he reaches down to help me up. Then he takes a ring of keys from his pocket and says, "Turn around."

When I do, he unlocks the cuffs and slides them into his jacket pocket. "Get out of here."

"And go where?"

"It doesn't matter," he says. "Just don't be here."

I feel the blood creep back into my hands. I shake them out and say, "I think I'll stick around."

"Don't be an idiot."

"I have to know, and I've got nothing else to lose."

Nolan shakes his head. "Okay, Jake, it's up to you. I did what they asked of me and that's enough."

He walks around to the driver's side, and I follow.

"You're leaving me out here?" I ask. "What if they don't show up?"

Nolan laughs. "Then you should consider yourself lucky." He opens the door, stops, then turns back to me. "I don't know what they want with you, but you'd be smart to get as far away from them as you can."

"I'm not going anywhere."

Nolan frowns, then leans down and reaches into the car. He picks something up off the passenger seat and says, "You had this back at your house. I brought it along." He holds out my .38. "You might as well have it, for all the good it'll do you."

I stare at my gun for a moment, but I don't take it.

"I was going use it to get you to talk."

"Not everything works out the way we'd like, does it?" He pushes the gun toward me. "Take it."

I shake my head, don't move.

I know better.

Nolan smiles and holds up his other hand. "No tricks, Jake, just doing you a favor. I can keep it if you want."

I reach for the gun.

When my hand touches the metal, I hear a soft hiss then a loud snapping sound, like a branch breaking. Nolan jerks forward and something wet slaps against my face.

I close my eyes and step back.

The gun drops.

When I look again, Nolan is lying facedown on the ground. One arm is pinned under him, the other stretched out, twitching in the dirt. The left side of his head is open, and blood is spilling out in every direction.

I take another step back, unable to look away.

My mouth is open, but there's no sound.

All I hear is the wind.

- 25 -

I look down at my hands. They're covered in blood. There's blood on my clothes and in my hair. I can feel it on my skin and taste it in my mouth.

My heart is slamming against my ribs, and my legs are burning under me. Every instinct I have is telling me to run, but I can't do it.

I take a step back from the blood, then see a dark shape duck behind one of the trees in front of me.

A shadow moving between shadows.

Coming closer.

I drop down next to Nolan's body and try to focus. The wind is loud, but my breathing is louder. I hold it and listen for footsteps crossing the parking lot toward the car, but there's nothing.

That scares me the most.

I feel something wet under me, and when I look down I notice I'm kneeling in Nolan's blood. I start to get up, then stop and lean over and search his jacket pockets. I find his cigarettes and lighter, and I toss them aside and keep looking.

Eventually, my hand closes around a cold metal key ring. I pull it out, then step over him and climb into the driver's seat of his car.

My hands are shaking, and it takes a minute for me to find the key. Every few seconds I look up and scan the park for movement, but all I see are trees and shadows.

When I find the right key, I start the engine, shift into drive, and hit the gas.

The car lurches forward.

I turn the wheel hard, spraying rocks and dirt into the air, then head toward the exit, fast. I clip the side of a tree, and the branches slap against the window. I yell and try to force myself to slow down, but I can't.

The adrenaline makes it impossible.

Once I'm out of the park, I watch the mirrors to see if I'm being followed. I'm not, and the farther away I get from the park, the more I feel myself start to relax.

Out of habit, I turn south toward the university and home. After several blocks, I remember I'm covered in blood and driving a stolen police car.

Going home is a bad idea.

I pull off onto one of the side streets and park in an alley, away from any lights. I lean forward and rest my head against the steering wheel. My stomach is spinning, rising up into my throat. I swallow hard and try to push it back, but it doesn't help.

I reach for the door handle and lean out.

Nothing comes up but bitter strings of spit.

I leave the door open, feeling the cold air on my skin, and try to figure out my next move. All I know is that I have to get off the street, but I can't go home, and I definitely can't go to the police.

That leaves one choice.

I feel my pulse radiating through my jaw and realize I'm clenching my teeth. I open my mouth slow, then lean my head back and stretch the tension away before pulling out of the alley and heading west, back to the warehouse district.

– – –

The gate is closed, so I park in the lot across the street and shut off the engine. I don't get out of the car right away. Instead, I look up at the light coming through the second floor windows and think about what I'm going to say to Gabby. I'll tell him the truth, but after our discussion earlier, I doubt he'll believe me, and I'm sure he won't be happy.

I cross the street to Gabby's front door and press the black buzzer on the wall.

I wait.

No one answers, so I step back onto the sidewalk and look up at the windows on the second floor. The lights are still on, so he's home. He has to be.

I press the buzzer again then knock, hard, and I keep knocking until I hear footsteps inside. When I don't hear the latch, I knock again.

This time there's a metal click and the door opens a few inches. I see half a face staring at me.

"Who the fuck are you?"

"Where's Gabby?"

"I said, who the fuck are you?"

I start to tell him that I've had a shitty night and I'm not in the mood, but I figure that's obvious from looking at me. Instead, I say, "Go get Gabby."

At first I don't think he's going to move. Then the face disappears and the door swings open.

I step inside.

The face turns out to be one of the guys I saw in the basement when I came out of the elevator. He's wearing the same shoulder holster, but this time the gun is in his hand, hanging at his side.

"You were here earlier."

I tell him I was and that I need to talk to Gabby.

I tell him it's important.

He looks at my face, then down at my shirt and says, "Is that your blood?"

"Some of it."

He seems to think about this. Then he slides the gun back into the shoulder holster and says, "You know you don't just show up over here like this."

"I know," I say. "Is he here?"

The kid motions to the stairs on the other side of the workshop. "Everyone is here. There's been a lot of excitement tonight."

I walk past him, through the workshop and up the stairs. I make it halfway before the door at the top opens and Gabby looks down at me.

"What happened to you?"

"Nolan."

Gabby's eyes go wide, and I can almost see the tension building inside him. I talk fast.

"He was in my house when I got home. He was waiting for me."

I'm expecting him to explode, but he doesn't. He doesn't even look surprised.

"Where is he now?"

"Dead."

This time, he is surprised.

He steps back from the door and looks down at his feet. When he comes back to me, he says, "Just tell me it wasn't you."

"It wasn't me."

I don't think he's convinced, so I start at the beginning. I tell him about finding Nolan in my house and him breaking my nose and driving me out to the park. I tell him what he said about the two men in the basement, how it was all an act, then about him unlocking the cuffs and letting me go. Finally, I tell him about the gunshot and seeing Nolan fall.

"You didn't see who it was?"

"I saw a shadow, that's it."

Gabby looks at my nose, one side to the other, then he moves away from the door and lets me inside.

I walk into the hall. There are several people sitting in the living room. None of them look familiar. A few are talking, but they all stop when they see me.

I figure I must look pretty bad.

I ask Gabby, "What's going on?"

He closes the door, says, "I want to hear everything Nolan said, especially about those two fucks we had in the basement."

There's an edge to his voice that I don't like, and I wonder if I made the right decision coming back.

I tell him everything.

As I go over my conversation with Nolan, everyone in the other room is quiet. They're all listening.

Gabby waits for me to finish then says, "An act?"

"He said they only told us what they wanted us to know, but I don't believe it."

Gabby is quiet for a moment. Then he waves toward the hallway and says, "Go get cleaned up. We'll find you some clothes, then we'll figure out what we're going to do next." He takes Nolan's keys from my hand. "Did you park across the street?"

I nod.

Gabby tosses the keys to one of the men in the living room and says, "The lot across the street. Get it and pull it around back."

The man turns and is gone.

"What's going on?" I ask. "Who are all these people?"

"Friends," Gabby says. "I asked for their help."

"What happened?"

"Kevin's missing. He left to drop those two friends of yours at the hospital and never came back. We've got people out looking for him, but I haven't heard a word."

I feel a pinprick of ice form in my chest.

It starts to grow.

Gabby looks at me. "Do you know anything else about those two? Anything you're not telling me?"

"No," I say. "Nothing."

Gabby nods. "There are a lot of eyes out looking for Kevin. If he doesn't show up soon, they're going to start looking for your friends." He stares at me. "If I bring them back here, they won't leave."

"I thought you wouldn't cross that line anymore."

"Yeah," Gabby says. "Me too."

– 26 –

I stand under the shower and let the water rinse the blood off my skin. It gathers red at my feet, then trails away toward the drain. I watch until it runs clear.

It takes a long time.

Eventually, I get out and wrap a towel around my waist. All my muscles feel weak, and my stomach is rolling. I lean against the sink until it passes, then reach up and wipe the steam from the mirror with my hand.

I stare at myself for a long time.

My nose is black and swollen. There are purple bruises on either side that spread like legs under my eyes. My nostrils are caked with dried blood, and when I try to breathe, I feel something loose rattle deep inside my head.

There's no doubt my nose is broken.

Someone knocks at the door, and I open it.

Gabby is standing in the hall holding a pair of pants and a white T-shirt. He hands them to me. "These should fit, give them a try. When you're ready, come out to the living room. We need to go over our plan."

"Our plan?"

Gabby nods, then walks away.

- - -

I get dressed, then gather up my bloodstained clothes and carry them out to the living room. Everyone is gone except for Gabby who is leaning over the coffee table with a roll of tape, some gauze, and a pair of scissors.

The TV is playing the local news.

Gabby is tearing off strips of tape and lining them up along the edge of the table. When he sees me, he motions to the chair next to him and says, "Have a seat. Let me take a look at your nose."

I hold up my bloodstained clothes. "What do you want me to do with these?"

"There's a trash bag in the kitchen. Put them inside. We'll worry about them later." He pauses. "And grab that towel by the sink."

I go into the kitchen and find the trash bag sitting on the counter. I put my clothes inside then tie the bag closed and set it in the corner. I can hear the news anchor's voice on TV, bright and emotionless.

I grab the dishtowel by the sink then walk back to the living room and sit in the chair next to Gabby. "Are they saying anything?"

"Nothing important. It probably won't make the news until tomorrow." He picks up the scissors and cuts a long strip of gauze. "Lean forward a little."

I do.

Gabby takes the towel and drapes it over my lap. Then he puts one hand behind my head and picks up a folded strip of gauze with the other. He holds the gauze over the bridge of my nose and feels along both sides of the break with his fingertips.

He doesn't say a word.

I ask him what he's doing, but he stays quiet.

I'm about to ask again when he squeezes my nose, hard.

The pain is blinding, and I hear something pop in the middle of my head. I make a sound deep in the back of my throat and try to pull away, but Gabby holds me in place and won't let me move.

"Be still, goddamn it."

My eyes are watering, and I can feel the blood running down my face and dripping onto the towel. I curse myself for not seeing this coming.

Gabby lets go of the back of my head, then reaches for one of the strips of tape on the table. He runs it across the top of the gauze and presses it tight. He uses another strip along the bottom and two more on the sides. Once they're all in place, he sits back and examines his work.

"Looks good," he says. "Couple months from now, no one will be able to tell it was ever broken."

"You could've warned me."

"Why, so it would've hurt less?"

"It's the principle of it."

Gabby shakes his head. "The principle." He laughs to himself then reaches for his cigarettes on the table. He lights one and watches me through the swell of smoke.

My nose is throbbing under the bandage. I try to ignore the pain and move past it, but I can't.

"Where did everyone go?"

Gabby takes a drag off his cigarette then reaches up and picks a piece of tobacco off his tongue. "Someone spotted the van. They found it parked down by the river."

"Kevin?"

Gabby shakes his head. "No sign of him."

I let some time pass, then say, "I never should've come to you."

"Where else would you have gone?"

"That's not what I mean. I shouldn't have gotten you involved. I didn't know who we were dealing with."

"You still don't," he says. "But it doesn't matter. I've always looked out for you, Jake. Always will. You know that."

I don't say anything.

"I'm going to lend you some clothes and a suitcase. You'll sleep here tonight, and I'll have someone drive you to the airport in the morning."

"I'm not going to the airport, not anymore."

"I need you to lie low until we know what's happening around here. The best way to do that is to leave town."

Gabby seems calm, but I still make an effort to keep the edge out of my voice as I speak. After everything that's happened tonight, I know something bad is waiting just beneath the surface.

"No one saw me. The park was deserted."

"Good," Gabby says. "Then we can bring you back in a few days, once we're sure. Besides, don't you have business down there?"

I think about Lisa Bishop and say, "There was someone I wanted to talk to, but that was before. I can't leave right now. I have to keep looking."

"No. Too risky."

I start to argue, but the pain in my nose stabs back into my head. Even if I wanted to argue, I don't think I have the energy.

"Give it a few days. Go see her or don't, I don't care, just stay out of sight." He takes a drag of his cigarette, then uses it to point at me. "Might be a good idea to pick up a few prepaid cell phones when you get there. I'll give you a different number you can use to check in. Call me every day, then break the phone and throw it away."

"What for?"

"So I can fill you in on what's going on up here." He watches me, frowns. "Do you understand?"

"Not really."

"Then you'll have to trust me." Gabby leans forward and taps his cigarette over the ashtray. "Until I know what's going on and who we're dealing with, we all need to keep our heads down." He looks at me. "Can you do that?"

I don't want to admit it, but what he's saying makes sense, especially after what happened tonight.

"I'll lie low," I say. "For now."

"Good." He takes another drag off the cigarette, then crushes it in the ashtray and stands up. "You'll stay here tonight. There's a guest room on the other side of the kitchen. Get some rest. I'll wake you up early."

I push myself up and start back to the guest room. I take a few steps, then look over at Gabby. "When they found the van, was there any sign of those two guys?"

"Nothing, but we'll find them. It might not be as easy this time since they'll be watching for us, but we'll get them eventually. They're out there somewhere."

I head back to the bedroom.

They're out there somewhere.

For some reason, this doesn't make me feel better.

— — —

I walk into the guest room and close the door behind me. The room is warm and lit by two silver lights on either side of the bed.

There is a desk against one wall and a small, three-drawer dresser with a large mirror along the other.

I sit at the foot of the bed and look at my face in the mirror. I don't recognize my reflection, and I decide that's not a bad thing. If I'm trying to lie low, I've got one hell of a disguise.

I stay there for a while, letting my mind wander until my thoughts turn black, then I stand up and get undressed. I set my clothes on top of the dresser, then pull back the sheets and slide into bed.

I think about the first time I slept under Gabby's roof. I was twelve years old, scared to death. I remember Gabby handing me a cot and a wool blanket and telling me to set up in a room above the office. I did, and even though the air up there smelled like grease and the blanket was old and rough and scratched against my skin, I was happy to be there.

As much as Gabby terrified me, there were worse things out there for a kid. At least with him, I knew I was safe.

Now, almost fifteen years later, I wonder if much has changed. The cot and the wool blanket are gone, but as far as I can tell, that's about it.

I reach over and shut off the lights.

– 27 –

"Get up, Jake."

I open my eyes. The room is dark, but the light from the hallway cuts through. Gabby is standing at the foot of the bed, holding a suitcase in front of him.

"What's that?"

"I've got you three sets of clothes in here. If you need more, you're on your own." He sets the suitcase on the ground, then reaches into his front pocket and pulls out a money clip. He holds it up and shakes it in the air before tossing it to me. "You can pay me back later."

I pick up the clip.

It's packed with bills.

"How much is here?"

"About a grand," Gabby says. "It was all I had in the house, so it'll have to do for now."

"I don't need it. I have money."

"Take it anyway, just in case."

I sit up slow, but not slow enough. The pain from my nose splits through to the back of my head, and I close my eyes tight against it.

"I'll get you a new bandage before you go," Gabby says. "You're a mess."

"I'll do it this time."

"Suit yourself, but do it quick. Your flight leaves in a few hours."

He walks out, leaving me alone.

I push the covers away then slide my legs over the side until my feet touch floor. It's ice cold, and for a second it distracts me from the pain in my head.

Then it fades.

– – –

After my shower, I stand at the sink and replace the bandage on my nose. The bruising is darker today, deeper, but the swelling is down and the rattling sound when I breathe is gone.

I hear Diane's voice in the back of my mind telling me that with a new bandage and some clean clothes, there's a chance that even I might look presentable.

It makes me smile, and when I close my eyes, I feel my heart break all over again.

Once I'm dressed, I close the suitcase and walk out to the living room.

Gabby is waiting for me.

He's standing in front of the full-length windows with a cup of coffee in one hand and a cigarette in the other. Outside, the morning sky is a wall of color, orange, purple, and pink, as if the entire sky has become part of the sun.

I set the suitcase by the front door.

Gabby looks at me then takes a sip of his coffee and says, "Your ride is waiting downstairs."

"Any news on Kevin?"

He shakes his head. "There won't be any, either. That's not how these things end up."

"How about Nolan?"

"Not yet." He sets his coffee cup on the table. "Come on, I'll walk you out."

I grab the suitcase, and we walk downstairs to the workshop and out through the front door. There is a black town car waiting outside the building. I look past it toward the empty parking lot across the street.

"Where's Nolan's car?"

"I had it taken out to the lot," Gabby says. "One less thing to think about."

I nod, but I'm still worried.

By now, Nolan's cruiser has been stripped, burned, and crushed. It's either sitting in a corner of the lot, or it's on the back of a truck heading to some faraway disposal site. Wherever it is, I'm sure no one will ever see it again.

This should make me feel better, but it doesn't.

Gabby puts a hand on my shoulder. He reminds me about the cell phones and tells me again to call him once a day.

"We'll keep each other updated," he says.

I climb in the back of the car with the suitcase. Gabby shuts the door behind me and slaps the top of the car with his palm.

We pull away.

I don't look back.

— — —

When we get to the airport, I get out and check my bag at the curb. I notice a few people staring at my face, but I ignore them and walk through the crowded terminal toward the security gates.

I stand in line and get ready to be pulled aside and searched, but when my turn comes the woman working the gate only glances at me and says, "Looks like it hurt."

"It wasn't too bad."

She smiles and waves me through.

I don't question it.

They probably figure that if I wanted to cause trouble, I wouldn't show up looking like trouble.

Once I'm through security, I walk down the concourse to my gate and find a seat in the corner where I can look out the window at the planes coming in from the east. I watch them land for a long time and try not to think about everything that happened the night before.

Instead, I think about Diane.

It occurs to me that once I'm gone, once I'm on the plane, there will be no reason for me to come back. When I get to Phoenix I can buy a jeep, then cross the border and head for the sea. From there, all I have to do is follow the coast until I disappear.

I let the thought take over. It warms me, and for a while I actually consider the possibility. Then it fades.

I can't run away, not yet.

Not without answers.

I sit up and look around. There is a bar across the hall, and I walk over and buy a bottle of water. On the way back, I see a line of pay phones.

I don't know if I'm making a mistake or not, but after everything Doug and I have been through, the least I owe him is a phone call.

He answers on the third ring.

"Hi, Doug."

There is a long silence, then movement and the sound of a door closing.

"You there?" I ask.

"Where the hell are you, Jake?"

"The airport," I say. "Remember that psychic I told you about? The one Diane saw in Sedona?"

"You're going to Arizona?"

"Just for a couple days. I'm going to need some time off." I pause. "I think I'm going to take Carlson up on her offer."

"A leave of absence?"

"Does the offer still stand?"

Doug sighs into the phone. "Of course it does. Take as much time as you need."

A woman's voice comes over the loudspeaker. It gives a flight number and announces boarding.

"I've got to run. My flight's boarding. I'll call you in a couple days."

"What if I need to get a hold of you?" Doug asks. "I don't think there will be any problems, but you never know. Anne might have questions."

"Can you cover me for a few days?"

"If that's all it is, sure." He pauses. "Is that all it is? A few days?"

I start to tell him it is, but for some reason the words won't come. Instead, I say, "I don't know."

"Where are you staying?"

"I'll find a place when I get to Sedona."

"Is she going to talk to you?"

"I don't know, maybe."

"Seems like a long way to go for a maybe."

I tell him he's right, it does.

"I'm guessing it wouldn't do any good to ask you to let this go, would it?"

"I can't let it go. You know that."

"Yeah," Doug says. "I guess I do."

- 28 -

I fall asleep on the plane and don't open my eyes again until we touch down in Phoenix. As we taxi to the gate, I sit up and stare out the window at a row of palm trees along the rocky brown hills.

This is the first time I've seen palm trees up close, and they're not what I expected. In movies, they're always full and green, bending and brushing against the wind. These are wilted sticks, like blown dandelion stems, desperate and weary under the constant sun.

Once the plane reaches the gate, I get out and head for the baggage claim. My suitcase is one of the last to appear. I grab it and go stand in line to rent a car.

The man behind the counter gives me several forms to fill out. I sign in all the right places and hand him my credit card. He slides it through the reader and sets it on the counter along with a set of keys and a map of the city.

"Enjoy your stay," he says.

I take the keys and the map and walk outside into the afternoon heat.

- - -

I follow the signs to I-10, then switch over to I-17 and head north. Once outside the city, the highway cuts through miles of rocky brown hills littered with saguaro cactus before flattening out into empty desert. A couple hours later, the desert turns green and rolls into hills.

When I get to the Sedona exit, I pull off the highway and drive into town.

Right away I see why Diane loved the place.

Every turn reveals something new, sharp spires and shadowed canyons, layered red rocks set against emerald-green trees, all of it framed by a warm turquoise sky.

The beauty of it makes me want to forget.

But I can't.

I drive through town until I spot a small hotel just off the main road. I pull into the parking lot and stop just outside the office. When I walk inside, the woman behind the desk looks up from her book and studies me over her reading glasses.

"Looks like you forget to duck," she says.

At first I don't understand, then I remember my nose and I do my best to smile.

"Car accident. Air bag didn't open."

"American car?"

"Why do you ask?"

"Because American cars are garbage." She turns down the corner of her page to mark her spot, then drops the book on the counter and moves to the computer. "I owned a Ford once, years ago. Nothing worked right." She looks at me and smiles. "Do you have a reservation, hon?"

I tell her I don't.

She nods and starts typing.

Her fingernails are long and painted pink. They rattle against the keys like bones.

"I can give you a room with a king bed, nonsmoking, of course. Will that work?"

"Perfect."

I watch her while she checks me in, then I look down at her book. The cover is red and glossy. There's a man and woman on the front, both half naked and windblown.

"Good book?" I ask.

"Nope."

I wait for her to go on. When she doesn't, I cross the room to the window and look out.

There's a long sloping hill behind the hotel, covered in scrub oak, and I can just see the silver blur of a fast-moving river through the branches. It's hypnotic, and for a moment, I lose myself.

Behind me, the woman rips a page from the printer and says, "I'll need a signature and a deposit on the room."

I walk back to the counter and sign the pages. I take Gabby's money clip from my pocket and peel off several bills and hand them to her.

She counts the bills then slides them into the cash drawer under the computer. "You're in room 217, at the far end." She hands me a plastic punch key. "If there's anything you need, go ahead and call the front desk. Someone's always here."

I turn the key over in my hand.

The woman picks up her book and opens it to the marked page. When I don't leave, she frowns. "Something else I can help you with?"

"Maybe," I say. "Is there a place around here where I can buy a cell phone?"

– – –

She gives me directions to a convenience store in town that sells prepaid phones. It's easy to find, and when I get back to the hotel, I drive around the side of the building and park next to the dumpster.

I walk up the stairs to the second floor and unlock the door to 217.

The room is hot.

I drop the suitcase on the bed, then switch the air conditioner to high and stand in front of the fan until the air turns cold. There's a desk in the corner, and I lay the cell phones across it in a row.

I bought three, one for each day I plan on being in town, and each with an hour of talk time. It seems like a waste to only use them once, but this is Gabby's plan, and I'm willing to go along for the ride, at least for a while.

I open my wallet and take out the number Gabby gave me, and then I pick up one of the cell phones and dial.

It rings three times before he answers.

I can tell right away that there's a problem.

"What happened?"

"What happened?" Gabby laughs, but it isn't funny. "Your face is all over the news. They found a fucking handgun in the park, registered to you."

I think of Nolan handing me my gun right before he was shot, and I feel my chest fold in on itself.

"They're calling you a person of interest, not a suspect, but that's bullshit. They're looking for you."

"Nolan took the gun from my house. He had it and dropped it when he—"

"You think that matters?" Gabby's voice is sharp, but I can tell he's holding back. "We have to move fast. Did you check into a hotel?"

"Yeah, I'm there now."

"Did you use cash?"

I tell him I did, and then I remember the rental car and close my eyes against the sudden flash of pain in my head.

I don't want to say anything, but I have to tell him.

Somehow Gabby already knows.

"What is it?"

"I rented a car," I say. "I had to use my credit card."

"Fuck, Jake. Why do you think I gave you the cash?"

"How the hell am I supposed to rent a car without a credit card?"

Gabby doesn't answer. He's not listening.

He's planning.

"The good thing is they don't know which way you went, so that should buy us some time to get you out of there." I hear him light a cigarette and inhale deep. "But don't use that goddamn card again, got it?"

"Got it."

"There's a guy in Flagstaff who owes me a favor. He's got a small plane. I'll call him and ask him to fly you over the border to Nogales, maybe set you up with a bus ticket south. I'll wire you some money, but that's all I can do until things calm down."

"I'm not going to run. I didn't kill Nolan."

"That doesn't matter."

"It's all that matters."

Gabby is quiet for a moment, then he says, "Come on, Jake. You know better than that."

He's right, I do.

"If you come back, they'll throw you in jail until they build a case. You won't find the people who attacked you, and you'll damn sure never know what happened to your wife."

I start to argue, but Gabby stops me.

"Just be patient."

"I don't want to run."

"And I don't want to see you go to jail."

His voice is loud.

Neither of us says anything else, and for a while all I hear is Gabby breathing into the phone.

"I'm trying to look out for you, Jake. If you don't want to do what I tell you, or you think you'll have a better chance on your own, just say the word."

I open my mouth to tell him I'll do it on my own, but the words won't come. If I'm going to find out what happened to Diane, I need his help. As much as I hate it, I know it's true.

"Okay," I say, fighting to keep my voice calm. "Where do you want me to go?"

- 29 -

Gabby gives me directions to a private airstrip outside Flagstaff and tells me to be there by midnight.

"If something changes, I'll call your room. Don't go anywhere until you hear from me."

I lie and tell him I won't.

After I hang up, I sit at the desk for a long time and go over my options. There aren't many left. It's only a matter of time before the cops trace my credit card and start looking for me in Arizona, so I need to move fast.

I didn't make this trip just to run away.

I open my wallet and take out Lisa's card. Then I pick up the hotel phone and call the front desk. When the woman answers, I give her the address and ask for directions.

Turns out, it's just a few miles away.

I grab the cell phone I'd used to call Gabby and walk down the stairs to the parking lot. I stop next to my car and look around for anyone who might be watching, then drop the phone on the ground and crush it under my heel. I pick up the pieces and toss them into the dumpster.

One down.

I get in the car and roll down the window. I can hear the soft rush of the river running behind the hotel, and I focus on the sound, letting it fill me before putting the car in gear and pulling out onto the street.

- - -

I follow the directions into the hills outside of town. Several of the street signs are set low and hidden by trees, but eventually I find the road I'm looking for and I follow it down a long hill that winds through a deep canyon into cool air and shadow.

The address leads me to a small brick house tucked in behind a wall of oak trees. There's a sign out front with the same moon-and-star logo that's embossed on the card, and when I pull into the driveway I can't help but think about Diane coming here only a few weeks before.

I shut off the engine and get out.

The air is damp and feels cool on my skin.

There's a rock fountain at the far end of the yard, and the sound of water cascading over the surface fits perfectly with the slow breeze passing through the trees.

I walk along a stone path to the house and climb the steps to the front door. I try to think about what I'm going to say, but nothing sounds right, so I decide not to say anything.

Today, I'm just another client.

There's classical music playing inside the house, and it stops when I ring the doorbell. I hear footsteps, then the door opens.

The woman who answers is small in every way. She's wearing thick glasses, and her hair is tied into two dark braids that fall forward across her shoulders. She looks at my face, and for an instant, a deep line forms between her eyebrows. Then it's gone.

She smiles, and I do my best to smile back.

"I'm looking for Lisa Bishop." I hold up the card. "It says walk-ins are welcome."

"Everyone is welcome."

She steps back and I go inside.

The house is larger than I expected. The ceilings are vaulted and cut with several skylights that give the room a cold, silver glow. There is a deep stone fireplace along the far wall, filled with burning white candles. The only furniture I see is a round coffee table surrounded by thick cushions.

"Nice house," I say. "Are you Lisa?"

"I am." She points toward the cushions on the floor. "If you'd like to have a seat, I'll be right back. Would you like tea?"

I tell her I would, then she turns and disappears through a beaded curtain. A minute later I hear water running, then the delicate clink of glasses.

I walk over to the cushions, but I don't sit down.

There are several paintings hung along the walls, mostly watercolors, desert scenes. I'm not an expert, but they look pretty good to me.

I stop in front of the fireplace and stare at a line of framed photos on the mantle. I go down the line, looking over each one, waiting for Lisa to return.

I start to move away when one of the photos catches my eye. It's a picture of Lisa sitting at a table in a dark restaurant with an older man. They're leaning into each other, smiling, and he has his arm around her shoulder. There's something wrong about the photo, something too familiar, but I can't place it.

Behind me, the beaded curtain rattles, and Lisa comes through carrying a silver teapot and two cups. She sets them on the table then runs her hands along her skirt, smoothing it out.

"I hope you like green tea," she says.

"I've never had it."

"Then I guess we'll see."

"Not today." I touch the bandage on my nose. "I can't taste anything."

"Well, that's too bad. Next time."

Lisa pours two cups of tea and holds one out to me.

I take it, then motion to the watercolors on the wall.

"Did you do these?"

"Oh no." She smiles. "They were gifts."

"From a client?"

"That's right."

I almost ask who gave them to her, but I catch myself before the question slips out. I have to be careful. If I'm going to find out what Diane told her, the last thing I want to do is scare her away.

"Do you mind me asking what happened?" Lisa touches the tip of her nose. "It looks painful."

I smile. "I thought you were psychic."

Lisa looks at me, and I can tell she's heard that before. "That's not the way it works."

"Sorry, bad joke."

She takes a sip of her tea.

"Someone broke into my house. They hit me with the butt of a gun, broke my nose."

"My God. I hope the police found him."

I nod. "They did."

"Good." She puts a hand on my arm and motions toward the coffee table. "Would you like to sit? Tell me why you're here?"

"I think I'll stand, if you don't mind."

"Whatever makes you comfortable."

I set the cup on the mantle then pick up the photo of Lisa and the older man in the restaurant. Once again, the feeling of familiarity hits me, but I still can't place it.

I hold up the photo. "Where was this taken?"

"Here in town," she says. "About a year ago. Why?"

"It's familiar."

I look closer.

There's something on the man's face. At first I think it's a shadow, but it's hard to tell.

"Is everything okay?"

I ignore her and move under one of the skylights, holding the photo up for a closer look.

I was right, the shadow isn't a shadow. It's a scar, smooth and pink, like a burn.

I feel my stomach drop and I step back.

"Are you okay?"

Now I see it, the deep-set lines around the eyes, the black hair splintered with gray.

I can't breathe.

Lisa touches my shoulder.

I tap the photo. "Who is this?"

Lisa frowns, steps closer. She doesn't take her eyes off mine until she's right in front of me. She reaches for the photo and says, "That's my dad."

"Your dad?"

She takes the photo and sets it back on the mantle, then puts a hand on my arm and leads me over to the cushions in the middle of the room.

"Why don't we sit down," she says. "You can start at the beginning and I'll see if I can help."

"What does he do?"

"Excuse me?"

"Your dad. What's his job? What does he do for a living?"

"I don't think my family is something I—"

"He's a doctor, isn't he?"

Lisa stares at me, doesn't speak.

"A coroner?" I step past her to the mantle and the photo. "I met him after my wife died. He needed me to identify her body."

"Mr. Reese, maybe this isn't the best time. I think you should come back another day."

"I'm not going anywhere. Who are—" I stop, look back at Lisa. "How did you know my name? I didn't tell you my name."

She touches my arm, and I pull away.

"Mr. Reese." She looks around at the front door, then back at me. "If you'd just sit for a minute, we can talk."

I start to ask her again how she knows my name, but this time she puts a finger to her lips, silencing me.

"You have to calm down."

"Who are you?"

Lisa steps closer. She lifts her face toward mine. At first I think she's going to kiss me, but instead she presses her cheek against my cheek and whispers in my ear.

"You need to leave," she says. "Right now."

I start to argue, but she squeezes my arm, tight, stopping me. When she speaks next, her voice is soft and steady, and her breath is warm against my skin.

"They're watching us."

- 30 -

I step back and look around the room.

"Who?"

Lisa shakes her head. "I'll walk you out."

"I'm not going anywhere." I move past her and through the beaded curtain into a small, sunlit kitchen.

Lisa follows.

The room is warm and clean, and there's no one inside.

"Where are 'they'?"

"Mr. Reese, stop. You don't—"

There are two doors at the other end of the kitchen, and I open them both. The first is a pantry filled with cans of food, and the other opens onto a wooden deck and large backyard. There is a thick jumble of trees beyond the grass, and a rusted metal swing set in the corner.

I slam the door and try to leave the kitchen, but Lisa steps in front of me.

"Enough," she says. "Leave or I call the police."

"Who's watching us? What do they want?"

"I can't. Not here."

"Why?"

She doesn't answer, and I push past her.

"Wait."

I walk back to the living room, then down the hall, opening every door I see, ignoring her.

Lisa pulls at me, but I'm twice her size and I'm not going to be stopped. I've come too far, and I've got nothing else to lose.

I open a door to a bedroom filled with candles and flowing curtains. There's a king-size bed against one wall with a shelf full of china dolls above it.

"I told you there's no one here."

"Where are they?"

"I don't know."

I cross the hall to the last door. This time Lisa manages to get in front of me, blocking the way.

"I'm calling the police."

"Who are they? Tell me."

"Not now. I can't."

I pull her away from the door.

It's locked.

I step back to kick it in, then hear a sharp metal click behind my left ear. I turn around, slow, and see Lisa holding a small black gun, pointing it at my head.

Neither of us moves.

"Are you going to shoot me?"

"I don't want to, but I will."

"Tell me who they are."

Lisa steps back, never lowering the gun. "Come on."

She leads me down the hallway to the living room. I ask her again to tell me what she knows, but she doesn't answer me. Instead, she motions toward the front door and says, "Out."

I walk to the door then turn back. "Were you part of it? Did you kill Diane?"

Lisa's mouth opens, and she looks at me like I slapped her. She shakes her head. "No."

"Then who did?"

Lisa looks past me to the front door. "Open it," she says. "Get out."

I open the door and almost walk out, but something won't let me.

"What are you doing?"

"There's nowhere for me to go. I have to know what happened to my wife, and you're all I've got."

Lisa adjusts her grip on the gun. For a second I think she might shoot me after all, but instead she says, "You shouldn't have come here. They let you go."

"Let me go?" I force my voice to stay calm. "What are you talking about?"

Lisa starts to say something else, and then the look on her face changes, grows softer. She lowers the gun. "You really don't know, do you?"

I laugh. I'm not sure where it comes from, but once I get started, I can't stop. "I have no idea what I know anymore, no idea."

I can tell she's trying to decide if I'm lying or not. Eventually, she makes up her mind. "The Church on the Rock. Do you know how to get there?"

I tell her I don't.

"You'll find it. There are signs all over town. I'll meet you in the parking lot at ten o'clock tonight and tell you what I know, for what it's worth."

"Tell me now."

"Tonight," she says. "And if you're not there, I won't wait for you."

I nod, silent.

"And don't come here again." She waves the gun at the door. "Now out."

I open the front door and step out onto the porch. I want to keep talking, I want to say something that'll make her understand, but I don't know where to start. It doesn't matter anyway, because once I'm outside, Lisa closes the door behind me.

A second later, I hear the deadbolt slide into place.

\- \- \-

I drive back to my hotel in a daze.

I went to see Lisa because I was looking for answers, but all I walked away with were more questions. Was I really being watched? If so, by who? And what did she mean when she said they let me go?

There are too many questions, but the thing that bothers me the most is the photograph of Lisa and her father in the restaurant. The same man who had me identify Diane's body.

It's too much of a coincidence, and I can't shake the idea that Lisa might've had something to do with Diane's death. If whoever is after me could get to Nolan, a police detective, it wouldn't be hard to get to a small-town psychic and her coroner father.

I wonder if I made a mistake by leaving. What if she doesn't show up tonight? What if whoever's watching her comes for her?

A lot could happen between now and ten o'clock.

I can't focus, and I end up missing my turn. I drive several miles out of town before I realize and have to pull over and double back. On the way I stop for gas at a station on the edge of town. There is a single red star on the sign, old and faded by the sun.

I stand at the pump and watch the numbers roll by. There's a warm breeze coming from the south, and for the first time since I left Lisa's house, I feel my thoughts start to slow down, and I begin to see my situation in a clearer light.

When the counter on the pump clicks off, I replace the nozzle and walk inside to pay. On the way, I pass a pay phone next to an ice machine in front of the building. Seeing it reminds me of my promise to Doug.

I try to ignore it, but I can't.

When I pay for the gas, I get change for the phone.

– – –

"Christ, Jake, the police have been here all day."

"What did you tell them?"

"What could I tell them? I don't know anything."

"You know where I am."

Doug breathes into the phone. "Must've slipped my mind when they asked."

I smile.

"I don't think I'll be able to explain this one to Anne," he says. "Not sure I'd even know how."

"I understand." I pause, then add, "You know I didn't kill anyone, right?"

"Of course you didn't. The entire thing is ridiculous, but Anne doesn't see it that way. If I look at it from her side, I don't blame her."

"What does that mean?"

"She's got the university to think about, and this is the wrong kind of press. This kind of thing doesn't help convince parents to send their kids to the school."

"It doesn't matter. I'm not coming back."

Doug pauses. "Where will you go?"

I lie and tell him I haven't decided, but my voice sounds strange, even to me. I think Doug notices, because he doesn't say anything right away.

When he does speak, he doesn't press.

He wishes me luck.

"I'll take it," I say. "All I can get."

I hang up the phone and walk back to my car. The sun is starting to set in the west, and the red cliffs reflect the low evening light and burn like embers against the sky.

I stand out there for a long time, watching.

- 31 -

I pull into the hotel parking lot, exhausted. I look at my watch. It's past seven, which means I have less than three hours before I meet Lisa.

Right now, all I want to do is lie down.

There are several cars in the lot that weren't there when I left, but I remind myself that it is a hotel, and most guests won't show up until later in the day.

It makes me feel better, but there's an uneasy buzz building at the base of my neck that I can't ignore.

As I cross the parking lot I hear the river in the distance, and the occasional car passing along the street. When I get close to the building, I notice a man standing alone on the second floor a few rooms down from mine. He's leaning over the railing, smoking a cigarette, watching me.

I walk to the stairs, telling myself I'm being paranoid, that he's just another guest. I don't know if it's true or not, but it gives me the strength to keep moving.

When I get to the top of the stairs, the man at the railing turns and looks at me.

"Evening," he says.

I nod and pretend to search my pockets for my key.

I walk by him, then look back to see if he's following. He's not. I don't see the other man until I get to my door.

He's standing at the far end of the walkway, hidden in shadows. I can't tell if he's watching me or not, but it doesn't matter. He's there, and that's all I need to know.

The buzz at the base of my neck starts to feel like an electric shock. I consider turning around and going back down the stairs to my car, but then I see the man with the cigarette staring at me.

My only option is to get into my room. If I can do that, I can buy some time to think.

I take the plastic key from my pocket and slide it into the lock. The light flashes to green, then red.

The door doesn't unlock.

The man at the far end of the walkway steps out of the shadow and starts toward me. I look over at the man by the railing. He takes a long drag off his cigarette then flicks it, end over end, into the parking lot.

I try the key again.

This time the light changes to green and I hear the lock click. I push the door open and go inside.

There is a man sitting at the table against the wall, facing the front door. He is older, wearing a dark suit with a blue tie. He doesn't speak, and he doesn't stand.

One of the men from outside comes up behind me. He steps into the room and closes the door.

I look at him and say, "What the hell is this?"

He doesn't answer, so I turn to the man at the table. "What's going on? Who are you?"

The man watches me for a moment, then reaches down and takes a briefcase from the floor. He sets it on his lap and flips the latches. "Have a seat, Mr. Reese." He holds his hand over his chair. "We have quite a bit to discuss."

I shake my head. "Not without a lawyer."

The man smiles, but there's something unnatural about it, something sour. Seeing it makes my stomach turn.

"We're not the police," he says. "And you certainly don't need a lawyer."

"FBI?"

The man shakes his head.

I wait for him to go on, but he doesn't.

"Should I keep guessing?"

A line forms between the man's eyebrows, then it's gone just as fast. "Of course, introductions." He motions to the man behind me. "This is Mr. Hull, and my name is Anthony Briggs. We represent a small, offshore company that I'm sure you've never heard of, and we need your help."

I look back at the man standing in front of the door.

He looks anything but friendly.

"I assume I don't have a choice."

Briggs smiles, but when he speaks, his voice is cold.

"There's always a choice."

We're both quiet for a moment. Briggs opens the briefcase on his lap. He takes out several files and sorts through them on the table, then picks one and holds it out to me.

"Take a look."

I don't move.

Briggs waggles the folder in the air. "I think you'll be interested."

I feel the man behind me step closer, so I start across the room toward the table, moving slow. When I get there, I take the file, but I don't open it.

Briggs shuts the briefcase and sets it on the floor. He sits back and crosses one leg over the other at the knee and says, "Go on, it'll help you make your *choice*."

I open it, but at my own pace.

I tell myself that no matter what I see, I'm going to keep my emotions in check.

It doesn't work.

There are a series of photographs inside, each one showing a different angle of Detective Nolan lying facedown in the gravel parking lot at Memorial Park. His head is open and wet.

Seeing the photos brings it all back.

My breath catches in my throat, and when I look up at Briggs, I can tell he sees it in my face.

"How did you get these?"

"We took them."

"Crime scene photos? You told me you weren't cops."

"We're not," Briggs says. "And these aren't crime scene photos in an official sense."

I look at the photos again, then close the file.

"I didn't do this."

"I know," Briggs says. "We did."

I look up at him. "*You* did?"

"We decided Detective Nolan had served his purpose."

"His purpose?" I step closer to the table. When I do, I feel a heavy hand on my shoulder, stopping me.

"We asked Detective Nolan to pick you up and bring you to the park." He motions to my face. "It looks like he got a bit overzealous."

I hold up the file. "They're blaming me for this."

"That was the idea."

His voice is casual, uncaring, and it catches me off guard. For a second, there are no words.

"We need your help, Mr. Reese, and this is our way of making sure we get it."

"By killing a cop?" I hear my voice rise, and I fight to keep myself calm. "Are you crazy?"

"Things were beginning to spiral out of control, due in part to Detective Nolan's involvement. All we did was step in to contain the situation." He pauses. "Unfortunately, things have become even more complicated than we expected."

"And you need my help?"

"That's correct."

I hand the file back to Briggs and say, "What exactly do you want?"

"The same thing you want, Mr. Reese." He points to my hand. "We want to find the person responsible for you losing your finger."

I smile. I can't help myself.

"Is something funny?"

I hold up my hand and say, "I've tried to figure out who did this since the night it happened. No luck."

"Then I think we can help one another."

"You're not listening," I say. "I don't know who did this, or why. If I did, I'd have found them already."

"Mr. Reese."

"I've gone over everyone I've ever known, and nothing makes sense." I shake my head. "I wouldn't know where to start looking again."

Briggs turns toward Hull, frowns, then looks back at me and says, "I'm afraid you don't understand. We already know *who* he is. The problem is finding out *where* he is. That's why we need your help."

This time I don't smile.

"You know who he is?"

"Oh yes," Briggs says. "And he's not from your past, Mr. Reese. He's from your wife's."

- 32 -

"You've made a mistake."

Briggs ignores me. He picks up another file, opens it, and takes out several photographs. He holds the stack up for me to see, then lays them out across the table, one by one.

I move closer.

The photos are of Diane, all candid shots taken through windows, while driving her car, or just walking along our street.

I go through them and try to ignore the tears pressing against the back of my eyes. When I've seen enough, I look up at Briggs and say, "What's all this about?"

"It's about your wife, of course, and you."

I stare at him, don't speak.

"Mr. Reese, I've worked with your wife for several years. You see, I'm somewhat of an art lover, and I found her to be an invaluable resource while building my collection."

"You were a client of hers?"

"A very good one, I'd like to think." Briggs picks up one of the photos, looks at it briefly, then drops it back on the table. "We trusted one another, and that's important when you're dealing with hard-to-find items."

"Hard to find?"

"Items that aren't necessarily legal."

"I don't understand."

"Works that have been listed as missing, or stolen, or perhaps lost in war," he says. "I find them, collect them, then resell them to others. It's quite a lucrative hobby."

"I didn't know that."

Briggs frowns. "That's surprising. I found your wife to be somewhat of an expert on the subject."

"You're telling me Diane dealt in stolen art?"

"Not exclusively, of course, but yes, if the opportunity presented itself, she did."

I nod and try not to laugh.

Not Diane.

Briggs keeps talking. I can't accept what he's saying, but I listen and shuffle through the photos on the table. One of them catches my eye, and I pick it up.

There's nothing special about it, just a photo of Diane walking down a crowded street, her hair pulled back and tied above her shoulders in a loose knot. She's staring straight ahead, calm and happy.

The look on her face is familiar, and it touches something raw inside me. I reach up and run my finger over the image, and the ache in my chest builds. I focus on it, thankful it's still there.

Far off, I hear Briggs say, "But that was before this latest incident. Now, unfortunately, things have changed."

"What incident?"

Briggs stares at me. "She didn't discuss any of this with you?" Before I can answer, he says, "Mr. Reese, how much do you know about your wife's business?"

"She was an art buyer. She worked part-time at a gallery in the city."

"Is that the extent of your knowledge?"

"What else is there?"

"More than you might expect," he says. "Did you know she worked with your father?"

This time I do laugh.

"Diane never knew my father. He died a few weeks before I met her." I start to toss the photo back on the table, but I change my mind and keep it. "You guys have really made a mistake."

Briggs takes a piece of paper out of the briefcase and hands it to me.

I look at it, say, "I don't know what this is."

I try to hand it back, but he doesn't take it.

"It's a copy of the visitor's log from Arrowhead Correctional. Your wife's name is listed next to your father's. She visited him in prison."

I look at it again.

He's right.

Diane's name is printed next to my father's, along with her signature. According to the date, she visited him a week before his heart attack, almost a month before we met.

For the first time, I feel a sharp ping of doubt in the back of my mind.

"I don't understand."

"They were business partners," Briggs says. "I don't know how often they worked together, but in this particular instance, Diane hired your father to hijack one of our trucks, the contents of which were quite valuable."

"You owned that truck?"

Briggs nods, doesn't speak.

"And you're telling me Diane was behind it?" I shake my head. "I don't think so."

"She didn't do it alone," Briggs says. "We looked into it and discovered someone inside our company provided her with the truck's route and shipment schedule. All Diane had to do was pass the information along to your father."

"I don't believe you."

"Not important. It is what happened."

I try to understand what he's telling me, but it doesn't makes sense. Diane wouldn't even cross the street against the light, and now I'm supposed to believe she was an art thief who helped my father hijack a truck.

No, I don't believe it.

"The heart attack was so sudden that we didn't have a chance to speak to your father after he was arrested," Briggs says. "We had nothing to go on until we checked the visitor log at the prison and found Diane's name. Once we discovered her role in this unfortunate event, we knew she would lead us to the traitor inside our company."

I turn and sit on the edge of the bed. "I don't understand. I thought you wanted my help finding the person responsible for cutting off my finger."

"That's exactly what we want. In this case, it just happens to be the same person."

I don't say anything, and Briggs stares at me for a long time. Eventually, his face softens, and he leans forward in his chair, resting his elbows on his knees.

"Mr. Reese, I understand this is a lot to take in, but I assure you it's all true."

"Why would this person want to cut of my finger?"

"I'm sure he assumed Diane was trying to push him out of the deal. You see, no one seems to know what happened to the cargo stolen from the truck. All he sees is Diane marrying you, the son of the man arrested, and he assumes he's been deceived."

"What about my father's crew?"

"Disappeared," Briggs says. "There wasn't much to go on to start with. Your father's face was the only one that showed on the surveillance cameras. From what I've heard, he was quite intoxicated."

"You should be able to find someone."

"Diane was our only lead. It wasn't until the incident with your finger that we knew for sure someone else was involved."

"You think he came after me to get to Diane?"

"That's our theory. Use her love for you against her."

I look away, silent.

"Honestly, Mr. Reese, we don't care about the cargo. What we're most concerned with is finding the thief working inside our company."

"And you expect me to help you?"

"You will help us."

"Is that right?" I shake my head. "I told you, I wouldn't know where to start."

"You'll start with your wife," he says. "I'm sure he's contacted her. Have her tell you where he is, then you'll tell us. We'll handle the rest."

I open my mouth to speak, but nothing comes out.

I clear my throat and try again.

"You want Diane to tell me where he is?"

"We have an idea where you can find her, but it's—"

"Is this a joke?"

Briggs stops talking.

"You want me to ask Diane?" I stand up. "Who are you fucking people?"

"Mr. Reese, please—"

"You *think* you have an idea where she is? I can tell you *exactly* where she is. She's in a goddamn urn on a shelf at Pearson's Funeral Home."

I feel a heavy hand on my shoulder, but I shrug it off. "I don't know who the hell you are, but you need to leave, now."

All eyes are on me. No one moves.

"Did you hear me?"

Briggs turns to the table and shuffles through the photos. He picks one up, looks at it, then hands it to me.

I take it.

It's a photo of Diane walking out of a building through a set of frosted glass doors and onto the street. She's wearing black baseball cap with her hair tied back in a ponytail.

I hand it back. "What about it?"

Briggs reaches out and taps the photo with his finger. "That photo was taken almost forty-eight hours ago, less than five miles from this room."

– 33 –

By the time Hull pulls me back, there is blood on my knuckles and my throat is raw from shouting.

"Who are you people?" My voice cracks. "She's dead. I saw her."

Briggs is down on one knee. He touches the corner of his mouth with one finger, then rubs the blood away with his thumb. He looks up at me, then pushes himself to his feet.

Hull has both my arms pinned behind me.

I keep struggling, shouting.

Briggs straightens his jacket and brushes his hand over his pants, wiping away any dirt. When he looks at me again, I open my mouth to yell at him. Before I can, he punches me in the center of the chest.

It's like being struck with a metal bat.

The pain splits me in two, and all the strength runs out of my legs. Hull lets go of my arms, and I drop to the ground. I roll onto my side and pull my legs up into my chest and try to breathe.

The pain doesn't fade.

Briggs takes a blue handkerchief from his pocket and touches it to his lip, then he bends down next to me and says, "It hurts?"

I want to scream, but I can't.

"Yes." Briggs nods. "All the nerves in the abdomen meet in this one location." He reaches down and touches a spot in the center of my chest. "Right here."

He presses, hard.

The pain is blinding.

I try to jerk away, but Briggs stays with it.

"These nerves can be quite painful when irritated." He lets go and pats my shoulder. "But don't worry, it'll wear off soon."

I'm finally able to pull some air into my lungs, but it feels like I'm breathing in shards of glass. I can't talk, and all that comes out is a weak moan.

"I understand your emotion, Mr. Reese, I do." Briggs stands and walks back to the table. "Maybe this is my fault for not making the situation entirely clear."

He picks up his overturned chair and sits down.

"Your wife's disappearance and the deception regarding her death was her doing, not ours. She lied to you just as she lied to us, and while I understand your embarrassment and your anger—" Briggs pauses. "I'm not the person you want to take it out on."

I get a hand under me and push myself up.

"I saw her body."

Briggs sighs and shakes his head. "Mr. Reese, I can assure you that your wife is alive. What I can't do is convince you, so I'm not going to try. Besides, we have more pressing issues to deal with at the moment."

"What issues?"

Briggs sits forward and says, "Two of our employees, the men who cut off your finger, actually, are missing. We lost contact with them, and we have reason to believe they've gone rogue."

"What?"

Briggs puts his hand on the table and starts tapping his knuckles on the surface. "They never should have been brought in on this. It was irresponsible."

I wait for him to go on. When he doesn't, I say, "What do they want?"

"The man we're looking for hired them to cut off your finger," Briggs says. "A foolish choice. A bit like using a shotgun to swat a fly in a crowded room."

"Where are they now?"

"No idea."

"Then how do you know they've gone rogue?"

Briggs looks at me and says, "There have been a few deaths."

– – –

"Their names are Mathew and Alek Pavel," Briggs says. "They were specialists in the Soviet military and came to work for us after the collapse. We hired them to oversee security for our export operation in West Africa during the Liberian civil war. They've been invaluable employees for years."

"And now they're bakers."

Briggs looks at me. "How did you know that?"

"Don't tell me it's true."

He stares at me, silent.

"I talked to them. The bigger one told me they came here to escape some mob and that they'd needed money to open a bakery."

"Escape from where?"

"Somewhere in Russia."

Briggs frowns. "What else did they tell you?"

"Lies," I say. "They told us what we wanted to hear."

"We?" Briggs leans forward. "I think you should start at the beginning. Who is 'we'?"

At first I don't say anything, but then the look in Briggs' eyes changes, and I realize keeping quiet isn't the best option.

I tell him about Gabby.

When I finish, Briggs doesn't look away.

"You're lying to me."

"I'm not."

"You expect me to believe this friend of yours was able to kidnap these men without incident?"

"Gabby has his methods," I say. "And it wasn't without incident. Before I left, one of the men who drove them to the hospital was missing."

"Dead."

"You're sure about that?"

"I'm absolutely sure. If what you told me is true, everyone involved is at risk. Including you and your friend, I'm afraid."

"Gabby can take care of himself."

Briggs stays focused on me, and I can see the smile in his eyes. "Did Alek tell you how his brother got those scars?"

I shake my head.

"I suppose how he got them isn't as important as what he did later," Briggs says. "Mathew was kidnapped by a militia who didn't approve of our company and what we were doing. They took him and tortured him. They cut out his tongue, then hung him outside for three days, letting the sun burn his skin black."

"Why didn't they just kill him?"

"They wanted to make a statement. I don't know why, perhaps because they're animals. Either way, they sent him home as a warning of our fate if we didn't agree to their rules." Briggs looks down and smiles. "It turned out to be a rather serious mistake on their part."

"What happened?"

"Once Mathew recovered, he and Alek and a few others tracked down every member of the militia, along with their families, and they destroyed them, one at a time."

"Destroyed them?"

"It's the only way to describe what they did," Briggs says. "There was no stopping them, even after the war ended and legal trade began. By that point they'd become a liability to the company, and we had no choice but to relocate them."

"So you brought them here?"

Briggs nods. "We set them up in the city, gave them a salary, and even helped them open a bakery. They're both very smart and actually quite civilized under normal circumstances."

I lean forward and push myself up off the floor. The center of my chest is throbbing and I still can't take a full breath, but at least I'm standing.

Briggs looks at his watch, then reaches into his jacket pocket and takes out a gold pen. He picks up one of the photos of Diane, flips it over, and starts writing on the back. "Once you get the information we need, call this number." He slides the photo off the table and holds it out to me. "I expect to hear from you tonight."

I look at the number then turn the photo over and stare at the picture of Diane. For a moment, I even let myself believe she's still alive.

Then I stop.

"Is something wrong?"

"I still think you're full of shit."

Briggs nods, doesn't speak.

"So that's it? I give you his location and all this is over?"

"We'll want to verify it, of course, but yes, tell us where we can find him and your wife's debt to us is paid. You'll *both* be free to go."

The anger is still twisting inside me, but I push it back and bury it deep.

"But keep in mind that we're not the ones you have to worry about." Briggs points at my hand. "They will be coming for you, so wherever you two decide to go after tonight, I suggest you find a place far away."

– 34 –

After they leave, I lock the door and sit on the edge of the bed and stare at the photo of Diane. I want it to be true, I want her to be alive, but I don't believe it.

I won't let myself believe it.

I drop the photo on the bed and ease back onto the pillows. My chest aches where Briggs hit me, and for a while the pain is enough to keep my mind off everything he told me, but soon the pain fades and my thoughts start spinning away from me.

I feel the tears coming, and close my eyes.

When I open them again, the light outside my window is fading. I sit up and look at the clock on the nightstand. I still have a little time before I meet Lisa, but the last place I want to be is sitting in my room, waiting.

I need to get out.

I push myself off the bed and grab a fresh set of clothes from the suitcase. Once I'm dressed, I take my car keys and one of the cell phones from the desk, then open the door and walk out into the dark.

– – –

I see the first sign for the Church on the Rock about a mile from my hotel. There's an arrow pointing the way, and I follow it up into the hills until I see another sign. From there it's easy to find.

There are no other cars in the parking lot, so I drive around back and park at the far end where I can keep an eye on the entrance. I sit for a while, waiting, and it's not long before my fingers start tapping and the buzz in my head becomes too loud to think.

I shut off the engine and get out of the car.

There's a brick path running along the edge of the parking lot. I follow it around the church to a circle of benches and a viewing area overlooking the town.

It's dark, and the breeze coming up from below is warm and gentle. In the moonlight, I can see the deep shadows of the valley stretching out toward the horizon and the scatter of red rocks silhouetted against the night sky.

I stand on the edge and look out for a long time, trying my best to stay calm. If I start thinking about Diane, if I start believing she's alive, I won't be able to think straight and I'll make mistakes.

I can't afford mistakes.

My stomach is twisted and raw. I try to keep my mind off it by pacing back and forth along the brick path, and focusing on what I want to say to Lisa.

A few minutes later I hear a car engine and see headlights coming into the parking lot. I walk back down the path, and when I come around the side of the church, I see a rusted white pickup truck stopped in front of my car.

As I get closer, I recognize Lisa in the driver's seat. She's alone, and even though I've tried not to get my hopes up, I feel them sink inside me.

Lisa sees me coming and rolls down her window. "What are you doing out there?"

"Waiting for you. There's a path—"

Lisa leans over and unlocks the passenger door. "Get in, let's go."

"Go where?"

"For a drive, so we can talk. That's what you want, isn't it?"

I walk around the truck to the passenger side and open the door. I notice a couple suitcases in the back, along with several cardboard boxes.

"You're leaving?"

"That's my business," she says. "Are you getting in or not?"

I look at the boxes again, then climb into the truck and close the door. Lisa pulls out of the parking lot.

We drive down the hill in silence.

— — —

"Where are we going?"

"We're driving." Lisa pauses. "This is the only place I know they're not listening."

I start to ask her about Briggs, then stop myself. If I tell her what happened at my hotel, she might decide it's too dangerous to talk to me, and I can't take that chance. Right now, she's all I have.

"Who are they?"

"No idea," she says. "All I know is that my phone is tapped and there are people outside my house who drive away when I come out."

"What do they want?"

"They haven't told me."

"If you had to guess, why do you think they're out there? Why are they watching you?"

"Why do you think?" She looks at me, then back at the road. "They're watching me for the same reason they're watching you."

"Diane?" I ask.

"That's right."

Something in my chest begins to vibrate.

"I wasn't a part of this, you know." She shakes her head. "No one told me anything. It wasn't until you started calling that I knew something had happened. The next thing I know, I've got people watching me through the trees outside my house."

My throat is tight, and I have to force the words. "Is it true?"

Lisa stares straight ahead, the light from the oncoming cars rolling over us both. "Is what true?"

"Is Diane alive?"

"How did—" Lisa pauses. "Yes, she's alive."

I look down at my hands. They're shaking, and I squeeze them together to make them stop.

It doesn't work.

"Where is she?"

"I don't know."

"Bullshit."

"No, it's not. I wasn't supposed to know any of this. I found out because of you, and I wouldn't let it go. I kept asking questions."

"Asking who?" Even before the words are out, I remember the photo on her mantle and I know the answer. "Your father. You're involved because of him."

"What do you know about him?"

"He was the coroner, the one who had me ID her body. He signed her death certificate."

Lisa nods, silent.

"Where is he?"

"Gone, God knows where. I haven't talked to him since he told me what he did."

"Since he told you he lied."

"Since he told me he helped her," Lisa says. "Just like he always does when she comes crawling back to him."

There's a hint of anger in her voice, but I don't pay much attention. I'm thinking back to the night in Fairplay when I identified Diane's body. Most of the memories are blurred, splintered by the booze, and they come back to me in jagged waves. The dark hallway and empty offices, the smell of ammonia, the way Diane's skin looked under the cold fluorescent lights.

"He never should've been involved, but Diane made him believe it was the only way." She looks at me. "How much do you know?"

"I don't know what I know anymore."

"Do you know how all this started? How she got in trouble?"

I think about what Briggs told me back at the hotel, but I decide to keep it to myself a while longer, just in case.

"I don't think so."

"Dad knew. He was the only person she told." Lisa frowns. "He wouldn't tell me what she'd said to him, but whatever it was, it worked. He dropped everything to help her."

"Help her how?"

"To start over," she says. "He helped her run away."

The buzz in my chest spreads through my arms, and I realize I'm holding my breath.

"I don't know how many favors he had to call in to pull it off, but he did." She holds up her hand and starts ticking off fingers.

"A death certificate, a new name, a passport, even a flight out of the country."

"A flight? She's gone?"

Lisa shakes her head. "I don't know, maybe."

I feel all the strength in my body fade.

"Why would he do all this? Why risk so much to help her?"

"Because she's a manipulator. All she had to do was tell him someone was trying to kill her, and he jumped to the rescue, just like he always does."

"I don't understand."

"He loves her, and that blinds him. He can't see her for who she really is."

"He loves her?"

"Of course he does," Lisa says. "She's his daughter."

- 35 -

"You're her sister?"

"Not by blood. Her mother and my father were close. Diane came to live with us after her mother died, so we grew up together. As far as I'm concerned she's my sister, even if she sees it differently."

"How does she see it?"

Lisa pauses. "Differently."

We're both quiet for a while, then I say, "She told me her family was dead."

"I'm not surprised."

"She said her father was in the military and she moved from base to base as a kid."

"That's true. He was an army physician, and we went where he was assigned." She smiles. "Did she tell you how many languages she speaks?"

"I didn't know she spoke any other languages."

"Four or five, I think. I don't know if she still knows them, but she did. It was a hobby of hers, that and her art."

We drive a while longer, and I listen to Lisa tell stories about what Diane was like as a kid. I find myself smiling, as if I'm learning about her for the first time.

Eventually the stories stop, and Lisa turns and doubles back the way we came.

I ask her where we're going.

"Back to your car."

"What about Diane?"

"What about her?"

"I need to see her."

"Good luck," Lisa says. "No one knows where she is."

"I thought you were taking me to her."

"When did I say that? I agreed to tell you what I knew, and I did."

"But she's here, she's in Sedona."

"How do you know that?"

I pull the photo of Diane out of my pocket and hand it to Lisa. "This was taken here, in town."

Lisa looks at the photo. "Where did you get this?"

Her voice is cold, and when I don't answer right away, she asks again, colder.

"There were a couple men waiting for me when I went back to my hotel this afternoon. They gave me the photo, and they told me Diane was still alive."

Lisa squeezes the steering wheel, tight, and the leather moans under her fingers.

I keep talking, going over everything Briggs told me about the hijacking and about Diane working with my father. I leave nothing out.

"Why didn't you tell me about this?"

"All they want is to find the guy who set it up, and Diane is the only one who knows where he is."

"And you believe him?"

I start to tell her I do, but the words don't come, and for the first time I really think about it.

Finally I say, "I have to believe him."

Lisa makes a dismissive sound then pulls off the road and hits the brakes, hard. I put my hands out and brace myself against the dashboard to keep from sliding down into the footwell.

"Get out," Lisa says. "Now."

I start to talk, but Lisa screams over me.

"Out, or I drive to police station and tell them you forced your way into my car."

"You can't leave me out here."

"I should've known better." She shakes her head as she talks, her voice distant. "I will not put myself at risk over this, not over her. I won't do it."

"Then tell me where she is. Help me find her."

"Get out, now!"

I watch her for a moment longer, and then I reach down and open the door. "Where do I go? Where's my car?"

"Keep walking, follow the signs."

I step out onto the side of the road.

"Some advice, Jake?"

I nod, wait.

"Leave, tonight," she says. "Let her go."

"I can't do that."

Lisa turns away, doesn't speak.

I close the door and watch her drive off. I wait until her tail-lights disappear over the top of the hill, and then I slide my hands into my pockets and start walking.

- - -

The road is dark.

I walk for a long time, ducking out of sight whenever I see headlights approaching. There's usually someplace to hide. When there's not, all I can do is lower my head and keep moving and hope it's not a cop.

I think about everything I learned tonight and try to put together a plan. The smart move would be to drive out to the airstrip in Flagstaff and meet with Gabby's friend, then fly over the border into Nogales and head south, never looking back.

But then what?

If everything Lisa said is true, if Diane is still alive, then I'm not going anywhere until I find her, no matter what the consequences.

I keep walking until the landmarks along the side of the road start to look familiar. Then I see one of the signs for the church up ahead and a white arrow pointing toward a dark road winding into the hills.

I cross over and follow the road until I get to the church parking lot at the top. My car is where I left it at the far end. As I start moving toward it, I feel a loose wave of nausea drip through me.

I have to make a decision.

Stay or go.

If I stay, I'll have to call Briggs and tell him what happened with Lisa. If I'm lucky, he'll give me more time to look for Diane. If I'm not lucky…

No.

I push that thought away.

I take the key from my pocket and slide it into the lock. As I open the door, I hear an engine, far off but getting closer.

I look up and see headlights pan across the trees lining the entrance to the parking lot. I duck behind my car. The headlights cover me, and there's no place to run.

All I can do is wait.

The car gets closer, and I lean over to look. The headlights are round and too high off the ground for a cop car. This should make me feel better, but it doesn't.

Not tonight.

The car stops in the middle of the parking lot. It's a pickup, a white pickup.

Lisa's white pickup.

I sit back on the ground and wait for my heartbeat to slow. When I hear the truck's door open and footsteps on the gravel, I step out from behind my car.

Lisa is walking toward me, a shadow in the headlights.

I say, "I didn't think you'd change your mind."

She stops, and I realize it's not Lisa.

The low buzz along the back of my neck kicks in again, spreading fast, through my chest and down my arms. I lift one hand to shield my eyes from the lights.

I barely realize I'm shaking.

She's standing right in front of me, but I still don't believe it's true. It's not until she takes a step closer, and I see her eyes for the first time, that it all comes crashing in.

"Diane?"

She watches me for a moment, then smiles.

"Hi, Jake."

- 36 -

Diane starts to say something, but I reach out and pull her close, cutting her off. She presses her head against my chest, and at first I think she's laughing, but when I look down, I see the tears.

She says, "I'm so sorry."

I touch the back of her head, soft, and don't speak.

"I never meant for any of this to happen," she says. "You have to believe me. Please tell me you believe me."

I do believe her, but the words won't come. There are too many thoughts rolling through my head, too many emotions, and I can feel myself shutting down.

Diane's shoulders shake, and the tears come even harder. I hold her and wait for them to stop.

Diane steps back and runs her thumbs under her eyes and says, "We have to go. The police are everywhere. They know you're here."

The words don't register right away.

Diane grabs my hand and squeezes. "Jake, we can't stay here. Someone is going to recognize you."

"How—" I stumble over the words, try again. "How did you do it?"

Diane pulls my hand, leading me toward the truck. "I can explain on the way, but we have to leave now."

She pulls again, and this time I let myself be pulled.

— — —

"Your picture is all over the news," she says. "They're looking for your car. We have to figure out how we're going to get out of here."

I watch her as she drives, unable to look away.

Her hands are constantly moving.

"Are you okay?"

Diane shakes her head and tries to smile, but she doesn't come close. "I thought this was over. I never meant for you to get involved."

"We'll be fine."

"I made such a terrible mistake. I was so stupid."

"We don't have to talk about this now."

"Yes we do," she says. "I tried to tell you the truth so many times, but I couldn't do it. I can't have any more secrets."

Her voice rises as she speaks, and I know the tears aren't far behind. I reach over and put my hand on her leg and squeeze. Slowly, I feel her start to relax.

I tell her it doesn't matter, not anymore.

"I didn't know what else to do. I thought if I was gone, if I disappeared, things would blow over and they'd leave you alone."

"You could've told me the truth."

"If I had, you would've tried to fix it." She shakes her head. "This one can't be fixed."

"So you just—"

"They were going to kill you, Jake, because of me." Her voice wavers. "I didn't have a choice."

There's still a part of me that wants to scream at her for what she's put me through, but mostly I just want to know how she did it. "You were alive."

"I'm sorry."

"When I was there, in the morgue, you were alive."

Diane stares out at the road, silent.

"And the coroner? Your father?"

"He set it all up," Diane says. "He knew everything that needed to be done, all the steps. He wanted to help."

I let her words sink in, and I don't say anything for a while. I know I should be angry, furious, but I'm not. I can't be. Diane is here, and we're together again.

This is our second chance.

"Where's Lisa? Why do you have her truck?"

"She's back at her house, waiting for me. She told me you came by this afternoon and that she agreed to meet you tonight." Diane looks at me. "You shouldn't have done that."

"That's what I keep hearing."

"It's dangerous."

"She told me she didn't know how to find you."

"She knew, but she thought I was gone."

"Gone?"

"I was supposed to leave tonight, but then I saw your picture on the news and I changed my mind." She hesitates. "What did you do, Jake?"

"I didn't do anything," I say. "At least not what they say I did."

"What about that detective?"

"I didn't kill him, but they're setting it up to look like I did."

"Who is?"

"A client of yours. A man named Briggs."

Diane's shoulders tense. She doesn't speak.

"He was at my hotel tonight, waiting for me. He told me a lot of things. Are they true?"

Silence.

"The stolen truck? My father?"

"I made a mistake."

"Who is he?"

"Briggs?" Diane shakes her head. "He works for a company called CDG Enterprises."

I tell her I've never heard of them.

"They're an American company that does a lot of charity work in West Africa: exporting food, medical supplies, clothing. It's all a cover for the import side of the business."

"What do they import?"

"Diamonds, mostly, but they'll deal in anything where they can make a profit."

"He told me about the stolen art."

"It didn't start out that way. At first he was just another client building a private collection. Everything he bought back then was completely legal."

"When did that change?"

"A couple years ago he asked me to fly to Buenos Aires and meet with a man who was selling his collection. He wanted to know if it would be worth his time."

"Was it?"

"No, nothing I saw had any long-term value. The man was in his nineties and had immigrated to South America after World War Two. When I told him we wouldn't be interested, he asked if he could show me one more painting. I didn't see the point, but Briggs wanted me to see his entire collection, so I went along."

"He had something valuable?"

Diane nods. "Very."

I wait for her to go on.

"He showed me a painting that was taken from a museum in Poland in nineteen thirty-nine. It had been missing ever since." She shakes her head with the memory. "I couldn't believe what I was seeing."

"And Briggs wanted to buy it?"

"I didn't think he would," she says. "When I told him the painting's history, I thought he'd want to report it, but I was wrong. From then on my role changed, and the money was too good to pass up."

"So what happened?"

"I made a mistake," she says. "A few months before you and I met, I was approached by a man at the company who'd figured out a way to steal one of CDG's diamond shipments. He asked for my help and I agreed."

"The truck."

Diane nods. "We got caught, and now here I am."

We both stare out at the road, and neither of us speaks for a long time. Then I say, "Briggs wants your help."

"My help?"

"The guy who set up the hijacking," I say. "They want to find him. He said if you tell them where he is, they'll leave us alone."

Diane stops at a red light and turns to me. Her expression doesn't change. "Briggs told you this himself?"

I take the photo out of my pocket and show her the number on the back. "He told me to call him tonight and tell him where he is. If it checks out, he said your debt to them will be paid and we'll be free to go."

"He said that?"

"Those were his exact words."

Diane looks back at the road. The light turns green, and we start moving again.

"What do you think?"

She shakes her head no. "The man they're looking for is Thomas Wentworth."

At first the name doesn't mean anything to me.

Then it does.

"The note on the jar," I say. "The body the cops found by the river."

"They don't need to know where he is. They tracked him down a long time ago."

"Then—" I stumble over my words, trying to understand. "What do they want?"

"They want their diamonds back. And once they have them, they'll come for me." Diane looks up, and all I see in her eyes is sadness. "There's no deal, Jake. These people never forgive."

- 37 -

Diane turns off the main road and takes side streets through town. She seems to know the way, but I'm completely lost.

I ask her where we're going.

"To a house in the canyon. I want to get off the street until we can figure out our next move."

I look at my watch.

"How long would it take to get to Flagstaff?"

"Not long. Why?"

I tell her about Gabby's friend with the plane. "He agreed to fly me into Nogales tonight. He can take us both, but we have to be there by midnight."

"Mexico? What are we going to do in Mexico?"

"Stay out of prison, for one thing. And if we're lucky, not get shot by your old boss."

Diane shakes her head. "Hold on, let's think about this for a minute."

"I have money, and Gabby said he'd wire more. We can figure out the rest once we're down there."

"How much do you have?"

"About eight hundred."

"That's not enough."

"It has to be. We can't stay here."

"Eight hundred dollars isn't going to do us any good."

"Then what do you want to do?" I can hear the impatient edge in my voice, and I make an effort to stay calm. "What's your plan?"

Diane taps her fingers on the steering wheel. "We keep going to the house in the canyon. My bags are there, we grab them, then go pick up Lisa. She can drive us up to Flagstaff and—"

"There's no time for that. Leave the bags, we'll buy what we need in Nogales."

"With eight hundred dollars? I don't think so."

I start to argue, but she stops me, says, "I have money. Not a lot, but enough to get us wherever we want to go, and we won't have to be in debt to Gabby."

I start to tell her it's too late, that I'm already in debt to Gabby, but I change my mind and don't say a word.

Diane looks at me. "All I have to do is run in, grab the bag. Five minutes, tops."

"If we're not there by midnight—"

"We'll be there," she says. "I'll be quick, I promise."

I'm not convinced, but the way she smiles at me is enough to make me give in.

- - -

The road into the canyon is dark, and Diane slows through the sharp turns. Once we get to the bottom, she looks over at me and says, "It's just up here a ways."

I look out the window, but all I see is darkness.

"Butch Cassidy hid out here," Diane says. "A lot of those old outlaws came here to hide from the law."

I mumble a reply.

Diane frowns. "What's wrong?"

"I don't like this, any of it."

"I told you, I'll just be a minute."

"It's not that."

"Then what?"

"How long did you work with my father?"

"Not long. He delivered paintings to a few clients from time to time."

"Stolen paintings?"

Diane hesitates. "Not always."

"Why would he turn on you this time?"

"He didn't turn on me. It was a bad plan from the start, and no one expected him to die."

"What was the plan?"

"Wentworth wanted there to be a chain," she says. "He wanted each of us to be responsible for the person under us. No one knew who else was involved."

"I don't understand."

"Wentworth brought me in. He gave me the shipping information, where the truck was headed, when it would arrive. It was my job to hire someone to stop the truck and steal the cargo."

"My father."

"It was his job to put together a crew to hijack the truck. Wentworth didn't know who I hired, and I didn't know who your father hired. This way if one of us was caught, there would be no way to connect it back to the company unless everyone talked."

"But if someone did, it would be like dominoes."

"Like I said, it was a bad plan. All we could do was hire people we trusted. This was how Wentworth wanted it, and he was in charge."

"And you trusted my father?"

"He never gave me a reason not to," she says. "He'd never let me down before. Even after he was arrested, he didn't talk to the police. He didn't talk to anyone at all."

"So, when you went to see him in prison, it was to find out where they took the diamonds?"

"His crew stored them somewhere, and he was the only one who knew where." She shakes her head. "I panicked. Wentworth was pressuring me, and I knew we were running out of time. It was a stupid mistake."

"That's when you came to me. You thought I'd know?"

Diane's quiet for a moment, then says, "At first, yes, but that changed after we met." She reaches over and touches the back of my hand. "When I said you gave me the courage to start over, I wasn't lying."

"Why didn't you tell me the rest?"

"I couldn't."

"You could've told me anything."

"I didn't think you'd believe me, and I didn't want to risk losing you. You were so set on not asking questions, leaving the past in the past."

She's right, and for a moment I can't think of anything to say. All I can do is wonder how things might've been different.

"I'm asking now."

"And I'm answering."

We're both quiet.

"If his crew has the diamonds, what's to stop them from keeping them for themselves now that he's gone?"

"They don't know what they have," Diane says. "I told your father they were stealing a shipment of rare statues for a private collector. He didn't know the truth, so his crew wouldn't have known either."

"Don't you think he checked?"

"If they did, all they found were crates filled with small statues, just like I told them. They're worthless, of course. The diamonds are packed inside."

"Inside the statues?"

"That's how they were brought into the country."

I lean back in the seat. "So, there are a bunch of statues sitting in a storage locker somewhere, and no one has any idea that they're worth—"

"Millions."

I look at her. "Millions?"

"Which is why we have to leave. Briggs has no intention of letting me go, especially if he doesn't get the diamonds back."

I don't say anything right away. I keep thinking about my father's crew sitting on millions of dollars' worth of diamonds and not having any idea.

Diane asks what I'm thinking.

"How many are there?"

"Sixty," she says. "Ten crates, six in each."

"What do they look like?"

Diane holds her hands about two feet apart and says, "They're about this big, white porcelain, shaped like birds. The diamonds are in velvet pouches, packed inside."

"Birds?"

"Doves."

For a second, I can't find my voice.

Diane hesitates. "Why?"

I smile. "Because I think I know where they are."

– 38 –

"Gabby has a statue." I hold my hands apart. "A ceramic dove about this big. He said it was a gift from my father before he died. He even offered to let me keep it."

She asks me to describe the statue, every detail. After I do, she says, "That has to be them."

"Gabby did the job." I shake my head. "Of course he did."

Diane is staring at the road ahead, not listening.

"Are you okay?" I ask.

"Does he know what's inside?"

"I don't think so."

She turns to me. "If we can get the diamonds from Gabby and give them back to Briggs, he might—"

"No, he won't."

"We have to try."

"You said it wouldn't matter."

"But what if I'm wrong? What if there's a chance?"

"It's too late for that. We have to leave, tonight. It's the only way."

Diane doesn't say anything else. She's still thinking about it, but for now at least, the conversation is over.

A few minutes later, Diane slows, then turns onto a dark driveway that curves toward a small brick house. There are no lights on inside, and when she shuts off the engine, the darkness covers us like a weight.

"This is where you've been staying?"

"Yeah, give me five minutes."

"It looks deserted," I say.

"That's the point." She opens the door and the dome light shines down, sharp and white. "I'll be right back."

I reach for her arm and she looks at me.

"We're going to be okay," I say. "You know that?"

Diane nods. "I know."

I let her go.

She gets out and closes the door. I watch her run across the lawn toward the house. Once she's inside, I step out of the truck and take the cell phone from my pocket.

– – –

The phone rings several times before Gabby answers.

"Jake, where—"

"Why didn't you tell me you were the one who hijacked that truck with my father?"

Gabby hesitates. "Who told you I was?"

"Diane," I say. "She was the one who hired him."

"What?"

"You didn't know?"

"He never told me," Gabby says. "You know what he was like. He kept all that shit to himself." He pauses. "So your wife, she's not—"

"No," I say. "She's not."

He makes a low noise, then nothing.

"Why didn't you say anything to me?"

"It never came up. That job was why I decided to retire. The entire thing was a bust. Your old man got picked up over a bunch of worthless statues."

"Yeah, we need to talk about those."

"Am I missing something?"

"You might be."

Gabby waits, silent.

I look up at the house and see a light go on in one of the rooms.

"Jake, you there?"

I start talking, filling him in on everything that's happened with Briggs and Diane. He listens, and he doesn't say a word until I mention the statues.

"Inside them?"

"She said no one else knew except the guy who hired her, and he's dead."

"Do you believe her?"

"There's one way to find out."

I listen as Gabby shuffles around on the other end of the line. A moment later I hear something break.

After that, silence.

"What is it?"

There's only the scrape of a cigarette lighter.

"Gabby?"

"I've got to go, kid. Make sure you're on that plane tonight. Midnight, no later."

"Was she telling the truth?"

"Yes she was."

He starts to hang up, but then I remember the Pavel brothers, and stop him. "The two guys in your basement. I know who they are."

Gabby waits.

I tell him the story Briggs told me about what happened to them in West Africa, and about what they did. "Now he thinks they're coming after us."

"Did he say anything else?"

"Nothing."

Gabby breathes into the phone, says, "Okay. Get on that plane and call me from Nogales."

"What are you going to do about them?"

"Don't worry about it. It's under control."

Then he's gone.

I hang up and slide the phone into my pocket.

There's an empty feeling in the center of my chest, and I can't help but think I might've started a war.

- - -

I look at my watch, then up at the house and see Diane pass by one of the windows. She's holding a phone to her ear, pacing back and forth.

It's been longer than five minutes, and my patience is slipping away. I cross the lawn to the front door, then lean in close and listen. I don't hear anything, so I turn the knob and walk inside.

The front room is empty and dark. There's an orange light coming from the hallway, and I hear Diane's voice in the distance. I look back at Lisa's truck in the driveway, then close the front door and walk toward the light.

I come around the corner into a wood-paneled kitchen. There is an amber bubble lamp on the floor next to a crumple of blankets and a stack of worn paperback books. Diane is leaning against the counter. When she sees me she hangs up the phone and says, "It's gone."

"What's gone?"

She waves the phone in front of her. "My bags, the money, all of it. It's gone."

The kitchen is attached to a small dining room with a sliding glass door that looks out onto a wooden porch. Beyond that, darkness.

"Lisa?"

"No." Diane shakes her head. "She couldn't have. It was here this afternoon when I left, and we have her truck."

"Who else knew you were staying here?"

"No one." Diane seems to consider this for a moment, then shakes her head and says, "No, no one."

"How much money did you have?"

"Twenty grand, plus. I know it wasn't much, but it was a start, Jake. It was our start."

Diane slams the phone on the counter then leans against it with her head in her hands.

I walk up and put my arms around her.

"We don't need it. Gabby can lend us—"

"You don't get it." She worms out from under my arm. "Someone was here. They went through my things and took everything I had."

"I told you, we'll get—"

"They know I'm here, Jake." Her voice is loud. "And if they know I'm here, then that means they're watching the house."

- 39 -

I reach for Diane's hand and lead her down the hall and outside to Lisa's truck. Halfway there, she stops and pulls her hand away.

"I can't do it, Jake."

"You can't do what?"

"Run like this, with nothing."

"Diane, I—"

"I don't want to have to look over my shoulder for the rest of my life. I can't do it."

"Then we won't," I say. "But if you're right and Briggs is watching this house, we need to go."

Diane looks up at me. "I'm going to tell them we found the diamonds."

"You can't do that. It's too late."

"Too late?"

"I called Gabby and told him what was inside the statues."

"You did what?"

"He had to know. If they track him down, at least he'll be ready."

"What did he say? Did he believe you?"

"He broke one open, saw for himself."

"Oh my God."

"Forget about the diamonds. Now that he knows about them, they're as good as gone."

"Call him, tell him the situation. If he knows you're in trouble, he'll have to help."

"Help how? You said these people don't forgive."

"But with the diamonds, there's a chance."

I look at my watch. "Our only chance is to be on that plane. We'll figure out the rest once we're far away from here." I hold out my hand. "You have to trust me."

Diane stares at my hand, then looks up at me and shakes her head. "I'm sorry."

A wave of light pans through the trees and over the ground. I look back and see three black SUVs turn off the main road onto the driveway, then spread out across the lawn. Their headlights are blinding.

"Get in the house."

Diane doesn't move.

I start to tell her again, then change my mind.

It's too late to run.

— — —

The SUVs stop, and all the doors open at once. Several men step out onto the lawn, moving between the cars, surrounding us on all sides.

Diane grabs my hand.

Most of the faces are dark, silhouetted against the headlights. I lift a hand to my eyes to block the glare and see Briggs and Hull crossing the yard to where we're standing. As they get close, Briggs holds his hands out and smiles.

"You found each other," he says. "How wonderful."

I feel Diane press against me.

I stay focused on Briggs and try not to look at the men surrounding us.

"We had a deal," I say.

Briggs ignores me and walks straight to Diane, never taking his eyes off her.

She whispers, "Jake?"

Her voice breaks.

I step in front of Briggs. "Hold on."

For the first time, he looks directly at me, through me, and I fight the urge to step back.

"You don't get to speak," he says. "Right now, I'd like to talk to your wife."

I open my mouth to say something, but Diane squeezes my hand, tight. "It's okay."

Briggs stares at me for a moment, then looks past me toward Diane, says, "Hi."

Diane doesn't say anything.

"Why don't you come with me. I'd like to talk in private, if you don't mind."

"No, she's staying with me."

"Is that so?"

"You and I had a deal. We—"

Briggs holds up one hand, stopping me. "Mr. Reese, I find it difficult to believe your wife hasn't explained the situation in detail. If I'm right, then you know perfectly well that there is no deal."

Diane pulls my arm. "Jake, don't."

"You should also know that we are quite serious about retrieving what was taken from us, and while I understand that you are little more than a pawn in all of this, my patience is wearing thin. I have very little tolerance for interruption."

"I won't let you hurt her."

"Commendable, but an empty threat."

I tell him again. "I won't let you hurt her."

Briggs looks at me, nods. "Let me see if I can make this any clearer." He leans in and whispers, soft. "Your wife is a lying whore, and unless she can make it right, she's going to pay for what she's done." He pulls back to see my eyes, smiles, then leans in again. "Any clearer?"

I don't say anything.

"It's not as if we didn't try it her way," Briggs says. "She was convinced you would know where they were. After all, it was your father who took them."

"We weren't close."

"Which is, I suppose, why her plan failed. Nevertheless, we tried her way. Now we try mine."

Briggs nods to the men on either side of us, and they come in fast, grabbing my arms and pulling Diane away.

She yells out to me, but there's nothing I can do.

"Leave her alone."

Briggs takes her arm and pulls her toward one of the SUVs, and they disappear in the glare of the headlights.

I don't see the first punch until right before it connects. The impact re-breaks my nose and vibrates through to the center of my head.

In the distance, I hear Diane scream.

The next punch catches me on the side of the face. I feel my teeth dig into my cheek and my mouth fill with blood. After that, they come too fast to count.

At one point, I realize I'm on the ground.

There are at least two men kicking me, again and again. Then it stops. I roll onto my side and pull my legs up to my chest. I run my tongue over my teeth until I find the one embedded in the flesh of my cheek.

I work it free and focus on the pain.

The darkness presses in, but I fight it.

Diane is crying, the sound far off and muted. I hear Briggs's voice, but the words are broken, and I can't put them together. A second later, one of the men kicks me again. This time the pain is far away.

Soon, everything goes dark.

- 40 -

"Wake him up."

I feel a soft hand on my cheek and hear a low murmur of voices. I open my eyes, slow. All I see are faded shadows moving around me.

I hear Diane's voice. "We have to go, Jake."

Several hands grab my arms and pull me up. I'm being half carried and half dragged across the yard.

I can't see Diane.

I hear a man's voice say, "Not that one. He'll bleed all over the seats."

Another car door opens, and I'm dragged away.

I feel the ground slide by under my heels, and then someone picks up my legs and I'm being carried. I lean back and look up at the stars spinning white through a solid black sky. I hold onto them for as long as I can, then I close my eyes and let them go.

- - -

"Jake?"

I hear a steady rumble, and I hold onto it, letting it pull me awake. I'm in the backseat of a car with my head on a towel in

Diane's lap. She's looking down at me and running her thumb along my forehead. Her eyes are swollen from crying.

"How do you feel?"

I try to speak but end up coughing.

When I stop, I notice Diane's hands are shaking. I reach for them and say, "I'm okay."

It's a lie, and we both know it.

I try to sit up.

"No, just lie still."

I tell her it's okay, then inch my way up to sitting and lean back against the seat. The pain comes from everywhere, but I do my best to hide it.

We're in one of the SUVs and there are two men in the front. One is driving, the other staring straight ahead. I see the driver look back at us in the rearview, but he doesn't say a word.

"Where are we?"

"Outside Flagstaff," Diane says. "We're driving to the airport."

"Where are we going?"

Diane fakes a smile and brushes the hair from my face. Some of it sticks to the dried blood on my skin, and I start to wonder how bad I'm hurt.

"I thought they were going to kill you."

I ask her again where we're going, even though I think I already know the answer.

"I told them about Gabby and the diamonds. I'm sorry. I had to do something."

Her hand feels warm and soft. I want to tell her not to be sorry, that I understand, but I can't find the words.

"They want you to set up a meeting. They want their diamonds back."

"What if I say no?"

"You can't say no. They'll kill you."

"Gabby won't just hand them over."

"They'll make him."

I smile and feel something pop in my jaw. I touch the spot, wincing.

"You need a doctor."

"I don't see that happening."

Diane watches me for a while, then leans her head against my shoulder, gentle. "Is this okay?"

"Yeah," I say. "It's perfect."

\- - -

We drive past the airport entrance and pull onto a service road by a large metal airplane hanger. There's a corporate jet idling on the tarmac out front, the yellow landing lights flashing.

We stop, and the man in the passenger seat gets out and opens my door. He looks in. "Can you walk?"

"I'll help him," Diane says.

The man nods and steps aside.

Diane touches my face. "I'll come around, okay?"

I tell her I can do it myself, but she's already walking around to my side. She takes my hand, and I slide out, feeling my bones settle into place.

Briggs and Hull are standing next to the jet's open door, talking, ignoring us.

"Nice plane," I say.

Diane holds my arm and leads me across the tarmac toward the jet. When we get close, Briggs motions us toward the steps.

"We'll join you in a moment."

Diane and I go inside.

There are two single chairs on one side of the cabin and a long leather couch on the other. Next to the couch is a dark wooden desk and a folding door leading to a private room in the back.

The air inside is cold.

There's a woman standing beside the desk. She watches me as I come in, and despite how I must look, the smile on her face never falters.

Diane helps lower me onto the couch and sits by my side. A few minutes later, Briggs and Hull come in and sit on the chairs across from us.

I ask them where we're going.

"To meet your friend," Briggs says. "I'm looking forward to the introduction. He sounds like a unique man."

Briggs opens a cabinet between the chairs and takes out three glasses and an unmarked crystal bottle half filled with an amber liquid. He pours three shots into the glasses, then hands one to Diane and one to me.

I don't take it.

"You won't have a drink?"

"I quit drinking."

Briggs nods. "That's wonderful, Mr. Reese, but if there was ever a time in your life to start again, this would be it."

I hesitate, then take the drink.

For a while, no one says anything. Then Briggs motions toward the woman standing at the back of the cabin. She comes forward, and he says, "Would you mind finding an ice pack for Mr. Reese?"

The woman nods. "Of course, sir."

She disappears through the folding wooden door leading to the back of the plane. Once she's gone, Briggs leans forward and says, "How are you feeling?"

"I'll be fine."

"Good, because I'll need you to play host once we land. I hope you feel up to it."

"Don't do that," Diane says. "Just leave him alone."

Briggs looks at her, smiles. "I'd prefer to meet this man after a proper introduction, a professional approach. Hopefully, we're not too late."

"What do you mean, too late?"

"The Pavel brothers," he says. "If they haven't gotten to him already, they will. After that, we believe they'll come for your husband."

I look over at Diane. Her face is pale.

"You have to call them off," she says.

Briggs laughs. "This has nothing to do with me, my dear. They're working on their own, and I'm afraid your husband brought this on himself."

"I told you where the diamonds are," Diane says. "We had a deal. You can't let them kill him."

"My relationship with the Pavel brothers has always been fragile at best. Their loyalty to me is strictly financial. Perhaps once our property has been returned, we can all sit down and come to some agreement. However, if something goes wrong, you and your husband are on your own."

Diane looks away.

Briggs lifts his glass and sips. "So you see, Mr. Reese, making this introduction is in everyone's best interests."

Outside, the jet engines start to spin.

The folding door behind the desk opens, and the woman comes out carrying a small blue plastic bag filled with crushed ice. She hands it to me, then turns to Briggs and says, "We're going to be taking off in a few minutes, sir. Is there anything else you need?"

"No," Briggs says. "Thank you."

The woman nods, walks to the front of the cabin, and closes the outside door. She leans into the cockpit and says something to the pilot, then turns and slides the privacy door closed between the cockpit and the cabin.

Briggs watches me.

"You're not drinking."

I lift the glass and finish it in one swallow.

He smiles. "Did you miss it?"

I look down at the empty glass. I want to tell him I didn't miss it at all, but I can't bring myself to do it.

"Yeah," I say. "I did."

Briggs picks up the bottle and removes the stopper. I hold my glass out, and this time he fills it half full.

"This is good. I'd rather do business this way. It's so much more pleasant."

"We should've tried it earlier."

"Perhaps," Briggs says. "But no point in regrets."

I take another drink.

The jet starts moving down the runway, slow at first, then picking up speed. Diane takes my hand and doesn't let go until we're in the air.

I keep drinking.

The alcohol tastes better with each swallow, and I have to force myself to take it slow.

No one talks, and for a while I think it's going to be a quiet flight. I close my eyes and try to rest, but a moment later, Briggs taps my leg.

"Okay, Jake," he says. "I'd like you to tell me everything I need to know about Gabriel Meyers."

- 41 -

Briggs asks questions for the rest of the flight, and I answer them all. It's easy to keep Gabby's secrets. He's kept a protective shell around himself for so long that talking about him is like talking about two different people with two different lives. I tell Briggs about one, and nothing I say is a lie.

When we land, Diane helps me up.

The woman who gave me the ice pack opens the door. We step off the plane and walk out into snowfall, the first of the year, heavy and thick. There are two black SUVs, identical to the ones we left behind in Flagstaff, and a Lincoln town car waiting for us on the tarmac. Several men are standing outside the vehicles, watching us.

Besides the snow, it's as if we never left.

Briggs pulls his jacket tight around his chest then turns to Hull and says something I don't hear. Hull nods and motions for Diane to follow him to one of the SUVs.

Diane takes my arm and we start walking.

"Not you, Jake," Briggs says. "You're with me."

I feel Diane's grip tighten.

I shake my head. "Not without her."

Briggs's shoulders lift, then fall with his breath. He steps closer. "I thought we'd made progress."

"I'm not leaving her."

"No one said anything about leaving her. She'll follow in one of the other cars. This will give the two of us a chance to talk."

"She comes with me, or I don't make the call."

Briggs frowns. He looks past us and nods.

I hear a metallic click and hear Diane's breath catch in her throat. When I look over, I see Hull standing behind her with a black pistol pressed against the back of her head.

Diane eyes are wide, glowing.

"I'm going to give you one chance to save her life." Briggs stares at me. "Only one."

I want to play it tough and tell him I don't believe he'll do it. But I can't. I do believe him, completely.

I let go of Diane's arm.

"Jake?"

"It's okay. I'll see you at Gabby's."

She's still watching me when Hull reaches for her arm. Diane pulls away, then starts walking toward one of the SUVs. Hull follows her.

I watch them go.

"For what it's worth," Briggs says. "I give you my word she'll be okay, as long as everything goes smoothly."

"That's not up to me."

"Maybe not." Briggs puts his hand on my shoulder and leads me toward the town car. "But I'm sure you'd tell me if you thought something unplanned might happen tonight." He pauses. "Especially with Diane involved."

I stop walking.

Every part of me wants to reach out and rip him apart, but each move I make sends jagged waves of pain through my body, and he knows it. I can't hide it.

"Do we understand each other?"

"If anything happens to her…"

Briggs holds up one finger and ticks it from side to side. "Let's not. It's such a waste of time."

He turns and walks toward the town car, leaving me behind.

I glance back at the SUV, hoping for one last look at Diane, but all I see are dark windows and the slow pass of the windshield wipers pushing away the snow.

Time to go.

I walk to the town car alone, feeling each step.

– – –

We drive away from the airport, and the two SUVs follow close behind. Once we're on the highway, Briggs reaches into his pocket and takes out a cell phone.

He doesn't say a word. I know what he wants.

I take the phone and dial Gabby's number.

"What do you want me to tell him?"

"The truth, of course."

I put the phone to my ear and listen to it ring.

When Gabby answers, I tell him what happened and that we're on the way to meet him.

"Where are you?"

"Half an hour away, at least."

He asks me who I'm with, and I tell him, then add, "They've got Diane in another car. They want you to return the diamonds, otherwise they're going to—"

"Don't worry about that," Gabby says. "Is he there?"

"Yes."

"Okay, do everything he tells you, and don't argue. When you get here, pull around back by the loading dock and I'll meet you outside." He pauses. "Let me talk to him."

"This has to go smooth. Diane is—"

"Don't worry," Gabby says. "I'll handle it. Now let me talk to him."

I hand the phone to Briggs.

Briggs puts the phone to his ear. "Mr. Meyers, it's good to—" He stops and listens for a long time. At one point he reaches down and runs his thumb over a spot on his knee. He smiles and says, "It's certainly something we can discuss." Another pause, then, "Very good. We'll see you soon."

Briggs hangs up the phone and slides it into his jacket pocket. He turns to the window, ignoring me.

"What does he want?" I ask.

"I'm sorry?"

"Gabby," I say. "He must want something."

"What he wants is irrelevant. He is a common thief, nothing more."

"He won't just hand them back to you," I say. "He'll expect something in return."

"We'll see."

I want to argue with him, but there's no point. What I care about is getting Diane as far away from all of this as possible.

Nothing else matters.

— — —

Once we get to the city, I give the driver Gabby's address and say, "It's in the warehouse district."

Briggs asks him if he knows the area.

"Yes, sir," the driver says. "I'll find it."

I watch Briggs across from me. He looks too relaxed.

"You're not worried?"

"About what?"

"You're driving into a situation you know nothing about. Gabby has the diamonds, so what's to stop him from getting rid of you and keeping them for himself?"

"Is that something he'd try to do?"

I consider lying, but there's no point.

"Of course it is."

Briggs smiles. "Not this time."

"You sound sure."

"I am sure," he says. "Mr. Meyers knows who we are, and he understands the situation. Plus, we have you."

I laugh but it turns into a cough, and I taste blood in the back of my throat.

"From what Diane tells me, you two are close. He won't risk you, which is why I wanted you to make the call. I wanted him to hear your voice."

"That doesn't matter to him. Gabby does what he wants, always has."

"I'm betting your presence will change that." Briggs motions toward the front of the car. "Do you see the man in the front seat? His name is Carlos. His only job tonight is to shadow you. He has no other duties."

I look at the man in the passenger seat. He's staring out at the road, and all I see is the back of his head.

"If anything goes wrong tonight, anything at all, then Carlos will kill you."

I don't say anything.

"After that, I'll give him your wife, along with very specific instructions to take his time, and to make it hurt." Briggs stares at me. "Do you believe me?"

My jaw is clenched so tight that it takes a minute before I can open my mouth to speak. When I do, I try to keep my voice quiet. I say, "I can't control what Gabby does."

"But you can explain the situation to him. If he understands what's at stake, perhaps he'll be less likely to do anything foolish."

"I told you, Gabby does what he wants. You're overestimating our relationship."

Briggs turns back to the window and looks out at the city lights and the slow falling snow. He hesitates, then says, "I honestly hope not, Mr. Reese."

- 42 -

Once we get to the warehouse district, I lean over and look out at the road ahead. The snow is falling heavier now, reflecting the headlights and making it hard to see what's coming.

Briggs asks if this is the way.

"It's just up ahead."

A few minutes later I see the sign in front of Gabby's warehouse, and say, "Drive up to the gate."

The driver looks back in the rearview.

Briggs nods. "Do it."

We pull up, and at first nothing happens, then a motor kicks in, and the thick metal gate slides open along a track in the cement. The driver waits until it stops, then drives in with both SUVs behind us.

There are two small U-Haul trucks parked out back by the loading dock. One is closed, and four men are loading crates into the other.

Gabby is standing next to the elevator smoking a cigarette, watching us pull in. When we stop, he drops his cigarette and crushes it under his foot, then walks down the steps and across the lot toward us.

"Is this him?" Briggs asks.

"That's him."

I open my door and slide out. My muscles are stiff from sitting for so long, and I brace myself against the car to stand.

Gabby sees me and stops walking, then he starts again, slower. The look on his face burns through me.

I move away from the door and Briggs steps out.

Gabby's face softens immediately, and for an instant, I barely recognize him.

"Mr. Briggs." Gabby holds out his hand. "We've got almost all the crates packed and ready to be moved." He motions to the trucks. "I split them up into two trucks this time, just in case, and I'd be happy to have my men drive them wherever you want them to go."

"That's not necessary," Briggs says. "We'll handle that ourselves."

Gabby nods. "I can't tell you how sorry we all are about this misunderstanding. I only hope we can move past it and build a—"

"How soon until they're ready to be moved?"

Gabby bites his lower lip, then turns and looks at the men loading the trucks. "Not long. If you'd like to come inside and get out of the snow, maybe we can discuss the other matter."

"The other matter," Briggs says. "Yes, why not." He nods at Carlos, then waves a hand toward one of the SUVs. Hull gets out and comes over. "We'll follow you."

I watch the SUV, hoping to see Diane, but I don't.

Gabby takes my arm, and we start walking toward the stairs on the side of the loading dock. Once we get to the top, we go inside and head for the door leading to the workshop.

Halfway there, Gabby's words drift to me, barely a whisper. "How many men?"

"Six, I think."

Gabby lets go of my arm. He stops at the bottom of the stairs and turns back to Briggs. "This is my workshop where we make the furniture. My apartment is upstairs."

No one speaks.

Gabby starts to say something else, but he stutters over the words and doesn't try again.

I've never seen him like this, and it worries me.

"Are you okay?"

Gabby ignores me, then starts up the steps toward his apartment. Once we get to the top, he leads us into the living room. Briggs and Hull sit on the couch. Carlos stays standing, his back against the wall.

"Would anyone like a drink?" Gabby asks.

Briggs leans back and crosses his leg over his knee. "Let's just get this over with."

Gabby nods and sits across from him in the leather chair. "Whatever you like."

I stand by the windows overlooking the city and the lot below. My muscles are stiff and bruised. I'm afraid that if I sit, I won't be able to get back up.

At first, no one says anything. Gabby rocks back and forth in the chair, absently tapping his fingers on his legs.

Briggs watches him and exhales long and slow. "What exactly is it you want, Mr. Meyers, or am I to guess?"

Gabby laughs, loud and fake. "I guess I'm a little nervous. I had no idea who was involved when we agreed to do the job. Had I known, I never would've taken part."

"But you did take part."

Gabby leans forward in the chair, and when he speaks, his voice is slow, pleading. "You have to understand, Frank Reese was a close friend. He asked me—no, he begged me to help. I couldn't turn him away."

"Because you're loyal to your friends."

"To the end."

"It's a worthy trait. Unfortunately, in this instance, your loyalty led you down the wrong path. You took the wrong job."

Gabby looks down at his hands, and I notice they're shaking. He folds them together in his lap, then glances from Briggs to Hull and back. He clears his throat, says, "I'm trying to fix the situation."

"For a price." Briggs smiles. "That's what all this is about, isn't it?"

"I've had those crates in my warehouse for months, taking up space."

"Your point?"

Gabby reaches for his cigarettes and taps one out, but he doesn't light it. "Reimbursement."

Briggs laughs.

Gabby takes the lighter from the table. He puts the cigarette to his lips. His hands are trembling.

"It seems only fair considering—"

"You stole my property, and now you ask me to pay a storage fee?" Briggs's voice gets louder with each word. "Is that what I'm hearing?"

"I think ten percent would be a fair—"

Briggs moves fast. I don't see the gun until it's pressed against Gabby's forehead.

"Hey!" I move in, then see Carlos step forward.

I stop.

Gabby closes his eyes and raises his hands in front of him, slow. He mumbles something I can't hear, then he coughs and says, "This isn't necessary."

"Do you actually believe I'd pay you anything?"

Gabby's lips are moving, but no sound comes out.

"The only reason you are still alive is because you're nothing. You're a hired hand." He leans in close. "You are labor."

Gabby nods, stays quiet.

"I'm going to walk out of here with the entire shipment you and your friends took from me. You will stay here and be thankful I let you live. That is the only deal I'm offering. Do you accept?"

Gabby clears his throat. "Yes."

"Good." Briggs steps back and lowers the gun. "I think you have enough to worry about with the Pavel brothers. If I were you, I'd focus my energy on that little problem. As you'll discover, they're a good deal less charitable than I."

Gabby blinks, once, then looks at me.

Briggs steps forward and says, "If that's all you wanted to discuss, Mr. Meyers, we'll go ahead and take the trucks now."

Gabby lights the cigarette, inhales. "The keys are in them."

Briggs and Hull start toward the stairs leading down to the workshop. Gabby watches them go, silent.

Carlos stays behind.

Once they're gone, I turn to Gabby. "What the hell is wrong with you?"

Gabby doesn't answer. He puts the cigarette to his lips, his hands no longer shaking, then gets up and walks to the window and looks out over the lot.

I ask him again.

Gabby turns and motions to Carlos standing against the far wall. "Who the fuck is this?"

I tell him.

"Why's he still here?"

"He was told to kill me if things went bad."

Gabby nods, takes another drag off the cigarette, and turns toward the bookshelves. "Do you want a drink, Jake?"

I shake my head. "I want to know what's going on. Diane is still down there."

"We'll get to her later, don't worry."

He takes two glasses and a bottle of scotch from the shelf. I watch him pour a drink. Everything about him is different, his body language, his voice, even the look on his face. All of it strong and steady.

I step closer, whisper, "It was an act, wasn't it?"

Gabby lifts the glass and finishes the drink in one swallow. He doesn't say anything.

"What are you planning?"

He sets the glass on the coffee table then opens one of the side drawers and takes out a silver handgun with a black suppressor on the barrel.

Carlos sees it too late.

Gabby fires one shot.

The bullet catches Carlos just beneath his nose, and a mist of blood fans out across the wall behind him. He falls backward, hitting the ground hard, his legs drumming against the wood floors.

I look over at Gabby, and for a moment I can't speak. When I find my voice, it comes out loud.

"What is wrong with you? They have Diane."

Gabby drops the gun on the chair, then grabs his glass and the bottle of scotch off the coffee table and pours another drink. "You sure you don't want one of these?"

I walk around the couch to where Carlos is lying. It only takes one look to know he's dead.

When I turn back, Gabby is standing at the window, sipping his drink, watching the lot below.

"Now they're going to kill her."

Gabby, still staring out the window, says, "It's time."

"Time? What the hell are you—"

He turns and looks past me toward the hallway. "Get everyone down to the basement. No one leaves."

I hear movement behind me, and I turn around.

Mathew and Alek Pavel are standing in the hallway.

- 43 -

Mathew Pavel walks past me and down the stairs. Alek stays behind. I look down and see the bandage on his hand.

He notices and smiles.

"Send up a couple of the guys on your way out," Gabby says. "We'll finish this tonight."

Alek stares at me. "What about this one?"

"He's with me," Gabby says.

The smile drops. "We didn't discuss this."

"That's because it's not negotiable."

"Everything is negotiable."

Gabby shakes his head. "No, he's not part of this, and he's leaving."

"I'm not going anywhere," I say. "Not without Diane."

Alek looks past me to Gabby and frowns. "What is all this? We had an arrangement."

"We still do. Nothing's changed."

Alek doesn't say anything else. He stares at Gabby for a moment longer before pushing past me toward the stairs.

I turn to Gabby. "What's—"

Gabby swings. His fist catches me under the jaw. It's not even close to as hard as Gabby can hit, but the blow still has enough behind it to snap my head back and send a cold jolt of pain all the way down my spine.

I brace myself against the chair. Gabby comes closer, fists clenched.

"What the fuck is wrong with you?" he says.

I reach up and touch my jaw.

"I'm doing everything I can to keep you alive, and you're doing all you can to fuck it up." He points one finger at me. "From here on, you keep your mouth shut. Got it?"

"Why are they here?"

Gabby looks past me at the empty doorway then reaches for his drink. "It's under control."

"Under control?" I stammer over the words. "What—"

"We found out where they were this afternoon," Gabby says. "But after you called and told me about the diamonds, I thought it would be better to talk to them."

"They want to kill you."

"Yes." Gabby nods. "But tonight we're partners."

"I don't understand."

Gabby grabs the second glass from the coffee table and pours the scotch. "We made a deal, Jake."

"A deal? As simple as that?"

Gabby hands me the glass, and this time I take it.

"Yes, as simple as that."

"Can you trust them?"

"Nope."

"Jesus." I walk to the window. Down below, the trucks are loaded and closed. Briggs is standing in the lot talking to Hull. I look for Diane, but I don't see her.

Gabby comes up behind me. "Do you have any idea how many diamonds are on those trucks?"

"I have to get down there, find Diane."

"It's hard to believe they were sitting in my warehouse this whole time." He laughs. "Your old man, Jake." He holds up his glass. "Here's to him."

I let him drink, then say, "Are you going to help me?"

Gabby looks at his empty glass, then turns back to the coffee table and the bottle. "I'm going to give you your father's share. It's a lot of money."

"Keep it, but help me get her away from them before they find out what you just did."

"Let them find out. It doesn't matter."

"They'll kill her."

Gabby laughs. "I doubt that."

"Is this a joke to you?"

The smile drops, and the way Gabby looks at me makes my skin cold. "Use your head, kid. They're not going to kill her. She's helping them."

"*What?*"

It's not true, I know it's not true, but hearing the words is like a punch in the chest.

"Diane fucked up and she's been trying to save her own ass ever since." He studies me for a moment, frowns. "You don't think this is all a coincidence, do you? Her working with your old man, then jumping in bed with you right after he died?"

"She explained everything to me. She made a mistake, and I believe her."

Gabby laughs, shakes his head.

"She thought I'd know where to find the statues. When she found out I didn't, she stuck with me. She's not lying."

"Come on, Jake."

"She married me. Do you really think she'd take it that far?"

"You were her best chance of finding them, her last chance. She rolled the dice on you, that's it."

I hesitate. "But she married me."

"They're worth millions." He lifts the glass and drinks. "A lot of women marry for less, and you know it."

I think back to the Diane I knew before the night I was attacked, before everything fell apart, and shake my head. "No, not her."

Gabby takes a deep breath and puts a hand on my shoulder. "Think about it. They could've grabbed her anytime they wanted. You were the only chance she had of finding those statues and saving herself. She knew it, and they knew it, too. She had to get as close to you as possible, and they let her."

"You're wrong."

Gabby shrugs. "No, you're blind. But it doesn't matter anymore. You've got your dad's share and you can do anything you want, go anywhere in the world."

"I'm not leaving without her."

"I'm doing you a favor, Jake."

I say it again, slower. "I'm not leaving her behind."

Gabby turns away. "What do you know about this company of theirs? CDG Enterprises?"

"We don't have time for this."

"It's not Briggs's company," Gabby says. "He wouldn't be here if it was, too dangerous. Most likely he's a field guy, someone who keeps things running smoothly."

"So what?"

"So, all this, tonight, is just us cutting off the snake's tail. They'll send someone else in his place." He pauses. "Unless we get lucky and he didn't tell anyone he was coming."

I can see where he's going, so I stop him and say, "He called ahead. All those guys down there met us when we landed. Someone knows he's here."

Gabby nods. "But they didn't know he was coming *here.*" He points to the ground. "You had to tell them where to go after you landed, am I right?"

I tell him he is, then add, "But you can't be sure."

"You can never be sure. It's all a risk."

"So what are you going to do?"

"I'll move those SUVs out to the yard tonight," he says. "They'll be crushed and shipped away in the morning. One of the U-Haul trucks goes to the airport with me. We'll unload the statues and fly them out."

"What about the other one?"

The look on Gabby's face changes, turns hard. "That one's not my problem. That one goes to the Pavel brothers. Part of the deal. Fifty–fifty."

"What about me and Diane?"

"You can come with me."

"With Diane."

"Jesus, Jake." He shakes his head. "If you want to kill yourself over her, that's up to you, but you're not going to fuck this up for me."

He starts to say more, but there's a knock at the door, and we both turn to look.

Two of Gabby's men come inside. They see Carlos lying on the floor and stop.

"No, not him. In the kitchen." Gabby looks at me and holds up one finger. "Stay here."

He walks away, giving instructions to the men.

I don't listen.

Instead, I stare out the window at the lot and the swirling snow, fading in from the black sky. I think about Diane, and what Gabby said. He might not believe her, but I do, and nothing he says will change that.

Down below, Briggs's men get into the two trucks and start the engines. I still don't see Diane. Every part of me wants to run down and find her, but if I go without Carlos, Briggs will know what happened and things will turn bad.

All I can do is follow Gabby's lead.

I stay at the window and watch Briggs walk back to the town car with Hull, and I feel my stomach twist.

I turn to the kitchen and start to tell Gabby that they're leaving. Then I notice the industrial gate at the lot entrance start to move, locking everyone inside.

I yell back, "The gate is closed."

No one answers.

I hear the three of them shuffling around in the kitchen, then Gabby's voice. "You got it?"

Something heavy hits the floor.

A minute later, Gabby comes back into the living room, swirling his drink in his hand. The two men follow him out, carrying the metal oven door that Gabby had hung on the wall.

For the first time, Gabby's plan starts to come clear.

"What are you doing?"

Gabby opens the door and watches the two men ease their way down the stairs, slowly. He doesn't look at me until the men are out and the door is closed.

"Where were we?" he asks.

"What are you going to do?"

"Only what needs to be done."

I start to ask about Diane again, but Gabby stops me. "I'm looking out for you, Jake, and you need to trust me. You're too close to see that she's lying to you."

"She's not lying to me."

"Even if that's true, she knows too much about me, and I don't trust her." He pauses. "I can't let her leave here tonight."

It takes a minute for what he's saying to sink in, but before I can say anything, I hear someone yell outside in the lot, then a gunshot.

I look out the window and see Gabby's men pulling everyone from the SUVs, taking their guns and leading them to the dock.

Hull is lying on the ground, pressing his hand against his stomach, trying to sit up.

Mathew Pavel is standing over him, watching. He's holding a gun in one hand. He lifts it, slow, then fires once into Hull's head.

The snow behind him turns dark.

I don't see Briggs, and I don't see Diane.

"You'll thank me one day," Gabby says. "You will."

I move past him.

He reaches for my arm. "Don't, Jake."

I pull free and grab the silver handgun off the chair where Gabby dropped it and head for the stairs.

I expect him to try to stop me, but he just stays at the window, sipping his drink, watching.

– 44 –

I hear several more gunshots as I hurry down the stairs, taking them two at a time. Every muscle in my body screams at me to stop, but I ignore the pain.

Halfway down my foot slips and I fall backward, hitting the stairs hard, then there's nothing. When I open my eyes again, I'm lying at the foot of the stairs, staring up at a dark ceiling, my vision fading in and out.

Gabby's gun is lying next to me. I reach over to pick it up, then feel hands on my shirt, lifting me, slamming me against the wall.

Alek Pavel is in front of me, holding me up. One of his hands moves to my neck, and I feel my feet leave the ground. I can't breathe.

He watches me struggle, silent.

I grab his hand and try to pull away, but my ribs shift in my chest, and I don't have the strength.

Alek's breath smells like peppermint and sour milk.

He leans in, whispers, "This isn't over between us."

My legs twitch, slapping against the wall.

I can't stop them, and I close my eyes.

Behind the slow rhythm of Alek's breathing, I hear a soft click. Then my feet touch the ground and he lets go.

I can breathe again.

I look up and see Gabby standing behind Alek with a small pistol pointed at a spot just behind his left ear.

For a minute, there's only silence. Then Gabby says, "I don't want to break our deal, but if you won't honor it, I won't have a choice."

Alek turns, and Gabby takes a step back.

"You will control this one," Alek says. "Or I will."

Gabby lowers the gun, slow.

Alek walks through the door leading out to the loading dock. He doesn't look back.

I lean forward, bracing my hands against my knees, waiting for my breath to return.

Gabby slides the gun into the back of his belt and says, "Come on, let's go."

"But Diane—"

He turns on me, fast, and I can't help but flinch.

"Enough! You stick with me, or you're on your own."

I swallow, taste blood. If I don't follow him, I have no doubt about what will happen. Right now, Gabby is my only chance of finding Diane and getting away.

"What's it going to be, Jake?"

"I'm with you."

He nods, then walks through the door to the loading dock.

I follow him, and when we step out by the freight elevator, my legs stop moving. No matter how hard I try, I can't take another step.

"My God."

Two of Briggs's men are dead, their bodies stacked on the loading dock just outside the elevator. Hull is still lying where he fell in the parking lot, and Alek Pavel is kneeling over him, searching his pockets as the snow falls soft around him.

I don't see Diane or Briggs.

"Where is she?"

Gabby presses the call button on the elevator, then looks up at the floor light above the doors. He doesn't answer me right away.

I ask again.

"Don't worry, they'll bring her in."

I look down at one of the men lying on the dock next to the elevator. His eyes are open, staring at me, his lips twitching. There is a wide hole in his stomach, and the blood leaking out looks black.

The elevator stops. Gabby pulls the doors open and steps inside. "Let's go, Jake."

It takes a second to turn away, but I do.

I stand next to Gabby as the elevator doors close.

Neither of us says a word.

- - -

When the doors open, the heat hits me hard, pushing me back. The air in the basement smells like gas, making it hard to breathe.

Gabby doesn't seem to notice.

I follow him out.

The sliding metal doors separating the main basement from the oven room are open, and I see the orange light from the flames climb the cement walls and cut into the shadows, revealing a spider web of pipes overhead.

Mathew Pavel is standing next to the oven with two of Gabby's men, all three trying to lift Carlos's body onto a metal rack in front of the open oven door.

I can't turn away.

Gabby walks to the desk in the corner, then takes the gun out of his belt and sits down. He runs a hand over his face and through his hair. He stares at me.

"How hard are you going to make this?"

I'm focused on the flames, and I don't answer him.

"You really don't see it, do you?"

In the oven room, the three of them manage to get Carlos on the rack, then slide him into the oven. Once he's inside, they close the metal door and press down on the handle, locking it in place.

"What are you talking about?"

"Your wife, Jake."

One of Gabby's men slides a lever on the side of the oven. There is a soft hiss of gas, then a low rush of fire.

I turn away and look at Gabby.

"Nothing you say is going to make me believe she's working with Briggs," I say. "Nothing."

"I shouldn't have to say anything to convince you."

"I should just take your word for it?"

"You're goddamn right, you should." He frowns. "Don't you think you can trust me, Jake?"

There's an edge to the question, and I know I have to be careful. "I trust you," I say. "But I know you, and you always have to be right, even when you're not." I hesitate. "And you're wrong about her."

Gabby laughs. I don't like the sound.

The light above the elevator flashes and the doors open. Two of Gabby's men are inside, standing next to three bodies. I feel my chest clench, and for a second I think one of them is Diane, but it's not.

I listen to the blood pulsing behind my ears and try to focus. I recognize two of the bodies as the men lying outside the elevator upstairs on the dock.

The third is Hull.

Matthew comes over and helps the other two pull the bodies out of the elevator and move them to the oven.

Gabby watches.

When they're gone, he looks up at me and says, "You need to prepare yourself for what's coming."

Out of the corner of my eye, I see his men lift one of the bodies onto the metal rack.

I already know, but I ask anyway.

"What's coming?"

The men slide the rack into the oven and close the door.

"You're leaving here alone tonight." He pauses. "I'm sorry, but it's out of my hands. There's nothing I can do about it."

In the next room, one of the men pulls the lever, and I hear the soft hiss of gas followed by the familiar hiss of fire. Something slams against the door, and an instant later, the screaming starts. The sound is flat, muted.

One of Gabby's men runs forward, reaching for the door.

Mathew holds out his hand, stopping him.

The screaming stops as fast as it started, leaving only the hollow roar of the flames.

The floor under me shifts, and I reach out for something to brace myself on.

"Are you listening to me?"

"He was still alive!"

"Yes," Gabby says. "And now he's not."

I want to say something, but the words don't come.

"You need to listen to me." He points to the oven. "If you don't, they're going to throw you in there and I won't be able to stop them. My ass is on the line here, too. I can't help you this time."

I open my mouth to speak, but my throat burns. All I can say is, "I can't leave her."

Gabby gets up and puts a hand on my shoulder. "But you will." He turns and walks into the oven room, leaving me alone.

Beside me, the elevator light flashes.

I step closer.

I tell myself that when the doors open, I'm going to make a run for it. I'm going to go back up and find Diane, then I'm getting her away from here, even if we have to jump the gate to get out.

The elevator stops. I close my eyes and breathe deep. All my muscles are tight, ready to go. Then the doors slide open, and I hear voices.

I open my eyes.

- 45 -

"Where is he?"

Briggs comes out of the elevator first, looking from me to the oven room. For a second, I think I see a flash of fear in his eyes, but it's gone so fast that I wonder if I imagined it.

"You." He points, moves toward me. "Where is he?"

I raise the gun and he stops.

"Think about this," he says. "You have no idea what kind of shit you're about to start."

"Where's Diane?"

Briggs stares at me, smiles.

It takes all I've got not to pull the trigger.

I start to ask again, and then I hear her voice.

"Jake?"

I look past him and see Diane coming out of the elevator.

The side of her face is red, and there's blood on her lip. I start toward her, but Briggs moves first. He reaches up and grabs the barrel of the gun, stepping to the side and twisting it out of my hand in one easy movement.

It's so fast that by the time I realize what happened, Briggs is up and firing, the metallic whisper punch of bullets tearing into Gabby's men.

I run toward Diane, grab her hand, and drag her behind the metal doors and into the oven room. Gabby and one of his men are inside, standing with their backs against the wall. The man is carrying a short-barreled shotgun. Gabby is holding a pistol. Behind him, Mathew Pavel steps forward, sliding a long clip into a black assault rifle.

I pull Diane into the corner, and we duck behind a stack of shipping pallets. "Stay down."

She nods, her eyes wide.

I look up and see Gabby nod to Mathew, then all three of them step through the doorway, firing as they go.

The sound of the assault rifle is rapid and loud, and it echoes through the room. When the shooting stops, I get up to look, but Diane grabs my arm and holds me back.

"It's okay," I say. "Wait here."

I come around the corner and see several bodies lying on the ground. Briggs is sitting with his back to the wall. There's a hole in his neck, and the blood pumps out in waves, rolling down the front of his shirt.

I hear Gabby say, "It's clear."

I start toward the metal door, but Diane stops me, says, "Don't, Jake."

I ignore her and cross the room to where Gabby is standing over the body of one of his men. As I get closer, I notice blood dripping off his hand onto the floor.

"You're hit." I point to his arm. "You okay?"

Gabby doesn't answer, just stares at the kid lying torn and broken on the floor.

I look around. Mathew is checking bodies, moving from one to the next. He stops in front of Briggs and bends down.

I walk up behind him. "Is he dead?"

Mathew shakes his head.

I hear Gabby pull the slide back on the gun, and when I turn around, he's looking at me.

"Bring her out here."

"We're leaving," I say. "You keep whatever you were going to give me. I don't want any part of this."

"Too late for that. Bring her out here, or I'll get her myself."

He starts through the doors toward the oven room, but I step in front of him, say, "I can't let you hurt her."

Gabby lifts the gun and presses it against my forehead.

I don't blink, just stare at him.

"Move."

I shake my head. "No."

A second later, I hear Diane come up behind me, and everything inside me shrinks. Gabby sees her and points the gun at her. I reach for it, then see Briggs shift against the far wall. He has a gun in his hand, and he lifts it, slow.

I yell, but it's too late.

Briggs fires.

The bullet hits Mathew Pavel in the side, just above his waist. He turns, backs up, then drops to one knee.

Gabby moves fast, crossing the room to Briggs and pulling the gun away. Briggs's arm drops to the ground. He sees me and smiles, his teeth coated in blood.

He coughs and looks away.

Gabby raises his gun and fires.

The bullet hits Briggs in the center of his forehead, and the force slams his skull back against the wall before dropping forward and settling loose against his chest, blood pouring freely into his lap.

In the middle of the room, Mathew is still on one knee, struggling to breathe. He sits, easing himself onto his back. He looks at

Gabby for a moment, then up at the ceiling, the shadows, and the orange light flashing in from the oven.

Gabby comes over and stares down at him, silent.

A minute later the elevator motor kicks on, and the light above the door flashes red.

Gabby sees it and frowns. "Oh, fuck."

- - -

The doors open, and no one moves.

Alek is alone in the elevator. He looks from Gabby to me to his brother lying on the floor. He steps out, never taking his eyes off Mathew.

When he gets close, he kneels next to him, blood spreading under them both. A second later, I hear a low growl coming from deep in his throat.

Every instinct I have tells me to run, but I can't move.

Mathew's body starts shaking. He coughs and blood sprays out of his mouth and runs down the side of his face.

Then he's still.

Alek stands, and I step back.

He starts toward Gabby.

The man with the shotgun steps forward and puts his hand on Alek's chest and says, "Hold on a—"

Alek doesn't look at him, just grabs his wrist and twists, hard, snapping cartilage and bone. The man screams. Alek slams his fist into the center of the man's throat. Something cracks, and the screaming stops. The man drops, silent.

Gabby lifts the gun, but Alek doesn't stop.

Gabby pulls the trigger.

It clicks empty.

Alek grabs him, pulling him off his feet, his arm around his neck. Gabby drives his elbow into Alek's chest and twists away, locking his arm in his.

Alek cries out in pain, and for a second I think Gabby has the upper hand. The way he has his arm locked, I'm sure it'll snap at any second.

But it doesn't.

Instead, Alek ducks down and sweeps Gabby's legs out from under him. They both go down, hitting the cement hard. Alek rolls on top of him and slams his fist into Gabby's face, over and over.

I hear the back of Gabby's head smacking against the cement with each punch. I run over to pull Alek away, but Diane comes up behind me and grabs my hand.

"No, Jake," she says. "Let's go, now."

She pulls me toward the elevator.

Alek stops hitting Gabby and wraps his hands around his throat. There is blood everywhere, covering them both.

Diane pulls harder, but I twist my hand away and grab Gabby's gun off the ground.

I hear Diane say, "Stop."

But I don't have a choice.

I can't let Gabby die down here, not like this.

I run up behind Alek and slam the butt of the gun against the side of his head, hard enough to make my ribs scream in my chest.

It gets his attention.

Alek lets go of Gabby and comes at me, fast.

I try to hit him again, but I'm not quick enough. He wraps his hand around my neck and slams me against the wall, his fingers digging into my throat.

I can't breathe.

Diane is behind him, screaming, hitting him.

He turns and slaps her, and I watch her fall.

The wall is smooth, nothing to grab. I try to pry his fingers away, but he only squeezes tighter, cutting off blood and air. I know that if I don't do something now, I'll never get another chance.

I lift my legs, bracing my knees against his chest, and push away as hard as I can. For a second, I feel his grip loosen enough for me to take in a breath. It helps, and I push my knees against him again, harder.

This time his grip slips, and I drop to the floor, hitting the concrete, gasping for breath.

The air burns, but I'm breathing again.

I only have time for a couple breaths before he's on me, pulling me to my feet. He slams me back against the wall, and the room spins around me. I can't focus, and I have no idea what's coming.

Then I hear the gunshot, and everything goes dark.

– – –

When I open my eyes I'm sitting on the ground, leaning against the wall. Alek Pavel is lying next to me. The back of his head is missing.

Diane is standing beside me, and I can already see the bruise forming around her eye. She's pulling my arm, begging me to get up.

Behind her, Gabby is sitting with the short-barreled shotgun on his lap, watching us. He is soaked in blood, and the light from the oven covers him like a shadow.

"Please, baby," Diane says. "We have to go."

I force myself up, then let Diane lead me across the room toward the elevator.

Gabby's eyes follow us.

Diane pushes the call button and the elevator doors slide open. Before I get in, I turn and look back at Gabby.

"I'm sorry."

Gabby watches us step into the elevator. Then he points the gun at Diane and pulls the trigger.

It clicks on an empty chamber.

Diane moans, the sound weak and tired.

He's still staring at us when the elevator doors close.

PART III

- 46 -

We take one of the SUVs and drive out of the lot and across town toward the university and Doug's house. I stay in the car while Diane runs up the driveway to the front door and knocks. The snow is falling heavier now, and she folds her arms across her chest as she waits.

I lean back and close my eyes.

When I open them again, Diane is standing at the passenger door, pulling me up, telling me not to fall asleep.

Doug is on the porch, watching.

I grab the edge of the door and ease myself up to standing, then we walk up the driveway to the house. Doug holds the front door open. Once we're inside, he leads us to the kitchen and I sit at the table.

Diane asks Doug for a washcloth.

"There's a closet in the hall," he says. "Towels, washcloths. Grab a few."

I look at Doug. "I'm sorry about this."

"Are you okay?"

I nod. "I think I look worse than I feel."

"That's good, because you look like shit." He frowns. "You need to go to a hospital, buddy."

There's no wink, no lighthearted comment, and that scares me more than anything. I try to smile. "Do I look that bad?"

"You want a mirror?"

"No." I shake my head. "I just need to rest for a while."

"Fine, but then we go to a hospital."

I hear a door open in the hallway and Diane shouts, "Can I use any of these?"

Doug tells her she can.

"No hospital," I say. "If I check in, the police will pick me up right away." I lean forward and cough into my palm. The pain shudders through me. "That's why we came here. There's a cop car parked outside our house."

"Maybe you should talk to them."

"Turn myself in?"

"You didn't do anything, right?"

"I didn't kill Nolan, if that's what you're asking."

"Then give a statement, answer their questions. If they can't pin anything on you, they have to let you go."

"There's more to it."

Doug waits for me to go on.

"It's not just the cops I'm worried about."

"Then what is it?"

"Gabby." I adjust myself in the seat. "He's looking for us. I think he's going to try to kill Diane."

"And there's my next question." He motions to the hallway. "You want to explain her to me?"

"It's a long story."

"I'm sure it is, but we've got time."

I start to explain, but then Diane comes back into the kitchen carrying a towel and several washcloths.

I look at Doug and shake my head.

"Are these okay?" she asks.

"They're fine."

Diane turns the water on in the sink and holds her fingers under the stream, testing the temperature.

Doug stares at me. "How can I help?"

"We need a place to go. Just for a while, until we can figure out our next move."

"You can't stay here. The cops came by this afternoon looking for you. It's not safe."

"No, not here," I say.

Doug frowns. "Then I'm not following you."

"You mentioned your place in Mexico."

"The beach house?"

I nod. "Would you mind?"

"I haven't been down there in a couple years. I've got no idea what kind of shape it's in."

"That doesn't matter. We just need a place to lie low for a while."

Doug leans back against the counter and folds his arms across his chest. "How do you plan on making it to the border? The cops are everywhere down there."

"We'll make it."

Doug turns to Diane at the sink and says, "It's an old house, hon. That's about as hot as it's going to get."

Diane runs a washcloth under the water, then kneels in front of me and starts wiping the blood off my face.

I reach up and take her wrist, soft. "I'll do it."

She hands me the washcloth.

For a few minutes we're all quiet. Then Doug pushes himself away from the counter and says, "I don't know, Jake. I think it's a bad move."

"Is that a no?"

"I didn't say that. I just think it's a bad move. Have you thought it through?"

"We have to go somewhere, the farther away the better. We'll figure out everything else once we've gone."

Doug pulls a chair from the table and sits. "It's late. Stay here tonight. We can talk in the morning."

"We should keep moving."

"I'll pull your car into the garage where no one will see it." He looks from Diane to me. "You can both get a good night's sleep. If you still want to leave in the morning, I'll give you the keys to the beach house."

Diane looks at me, shrugs.

"I want you to be sure," Doug says. "Because once you run, you'll have to keep running."

I turn to Diane. "What do you think?"

She takes the washcloth from me, touches it against my forehead, and says, "I think he's right."

- - -

Doug leads us back to a spare room and turns on the overhead light. "Bathroom's across the hall. You already know where to find towels." He points over his shoulder. "My room is down there if you need me. Get some rest, we'll talk in the morning."

We thank him and close the door. There is a double bed against one wall and a rocking chair in the corner. The room is filled with cardboard moving boxes and stacks of literary journals and magazines.

I sit on the edge of the bed and ease back.

"Are you okay?" Diane asks.

"Sore, but I'll make it."

Diane climbs onto the bed and lies next to me. "Take a hot bath, it'll help."

I tell her I might, but I don't move.

"Do you think what he said is true? That once we run, we'll have to keep running?"

"Probably."

"I don't think I can do that."

"We don't have a choice."

"What if we talk to the police?" She props up on one elbow and looks at me. "I heard what Doug said, and I think he's right. Maybe you should answer their questions. They can't charge you with something you didn't do."

I laugh. "Even if that were true, what would we do? Go back to our old life? I start teaching again, you go back to the gallery? Do you see that happening after all this?"

"It could."

I shake my head. "That life is over."

Neither of us says anything else.

Diane watches me for a while longer, and then she lies back on the bed. A few minutes later, I hear her crying, soft and quiet.

I roll over and try to sleep.

– 47 –

I open my eyes, and for a moment I don't know where I am. There's a thin strip of morning coming in through the break in the curtains, turning the room a cold blue. Diane is lying on the bed with her back to me. I sit up slow, trying not to wake her, then walk out into the hallway.

I hear the delicate sound of dishes coming from the kitchen, and when I turn the corner I see Doug standing at the sink, rinsing a coffee cup.

"Morning," I say.

He looks back at me, then points to the table. "Have a seat. Want some coffee?"

"Sure." I pull out one of the chairs and sit down. There is a silver ring of keys sitting on the table next to a folded map.

"I woke up early," Doug says. "Couldn't sleep."

I start to apologize again for dropping in so late, but he stops me before I finish.

"It wasn't that. I was just thinking about your situation." He motions toward the hall. "Is Diane still sleeping?"

I nod.

Doug reaches for the coffee pot and fills two cups. He hands one to me, then pulls out a chair and sits down. "I didn't ask many questions last night. I know you'll only tell me what you want to tell me, so I didn't see the point in pushing."

"I appreciate that."

"Well, you might not in a minute." Doug takes the key ring off the table. "These are the keys to my place in El Regalo. If you're set on going, I'll give them to you."

"But?"

"But I want to know what happened. I want to know why she's back and why you think Gabby wants to kill her. From what I know of him, he watches out for you, so why would he want to kill your wife?"

I don't say anything.

"Is it money?"

I sip the coffee and it burns. "Of course it's money."

Doug sits back and waits for me to go on. The house is still, and the only sounds I hear are the morning birds on the lawn outside the window.

"Where do you want me to start?"

"The last I heard of Diane, she was dead. Now she's not. Why don't you start there?"

I nod. "Okay."

I go over everything, trying to keep it all straight in my head as I talk. Doug listens, refilling his coffee cup once while I speak. He doesn't show any emotion at all until I tell him about the statues and the diamonds. Then his left eye starts to twitch.

"And Gabby wants to kill her because of the diamonds?"

"Because of the company that owns the diamonds," I say. "He thinks she's a loose end and will lead them to him if they come looking."

"It makes sense."

I hesitate for a moment. "He also thought she was working with Briggs. He thought she was using me the entire time to find the statues."

"And you didn't believe him?"

"Of course I didn't. I still don't."

"But?"

"What makes you think there's something else?"

Doug shrugs. "Tell me there isn't."

I pause, look down at my cup. "It does seems a little coincidental."

"You could say that."

I finish the last of my coffee then set the cup on the table in front of me. "But I trust her."

Doug stands and grabs the coffee pot. He refills my cup.

"Why don't you spit it out. I know you've got thoughts on all of this. Do you think Gabby's right?"

Doug shakes his head. "I don't know. Maybe."

"Maybe?"

"I'll say this. People might fake their deaths in the movies, but not in the real world, not like this."

"How do you know?"

"Because you don't just decide one day to do something like that. You can't just hit a reset button on life. It's not that easy."

"She did it."

"And that's what bothers me," Doug says. "She did it. She faked her own death."

"I don't see your point."

Doug puts the coffee pot back, then sits. "How would you go about faking your death? Any ideas?"

I shake my head.

"She knew how to do it."

"She had help."

"That doesn't make it better," Doug says. "Whoever did it knew what they were doing. They were able to arrange the entire thing. They were pros, and that worries me."

"Worries you?"

Doug leans forward and rests his arms on the table. "How much do you really know about Diane?"

"She's my wife."

"Can you trust her?"

"She's my wife."

"That's not an answer."

"It's my answer."

Doug leans back, doesn't speak.

"Do you think Gabby's right? Do you think it's all a lie, our marriage, our life together?"

"Do you?"

My immediate reaction is to tell him, "No, of course I don't, none of it was a lie." But no matter how much I want to say it, I can't do it.

Doug watches me for a moment, then he picks up the keys and twirls them once on his finger.

"You still want them?"

"Yes."

"Then they're yours." He slaps them on the table and slides them toward me. "Maybe some time alone, just the two of you, away from all this, will make things clearer."

I stare at the keys and don't say anything.

Doug picks up the map, unfolds it, and lays it flat on the surface of the table. "Here's where you're going." He turns the map so I can see. "El Regalo, right here. When you get there, talk to a man named Oscar Guzman. He runs the local market in town, and he takes care of the house for me. Everything in town goes through him. I'll write a letter of introduction for you before you go. Give it to him, and he'll help you with anything you need."

"You shouldn't do that. If we get stopped, they'll know you helped us."

"I'll take the chance," Doug says. "But that's as far as I'll go. Once you're down there, neither of you should try contacting me or anyone else back here for at least a month, maybe longer."

I nod. "It's a deal."

"Good." Doug sips his coffee, then looks back at the map. "Let me show you the best place to cross, and a few of the back roads you can take to avoid the police."

- - -

When Diane wakes up, we all sit in the kitchen, and I tell her the plan. She listens, sometimes looking at the map, sometimes staring out the window at the cars passing along the street.

When I finish, she turns to Doug and says, "Thank you for this."

"Don't thank me yet," he says. "Wait until you get across the border, then you can thank me."

"Okay, I will."

Doug pushes himself up from the table and motions for us to follow. "Let's see if we can find you two some clean clothes."

Doug has a lot of T-shirts. We borrow a few, then take a couple bottles of water and walk out to the garage and the SUV.

"Follow the roads I showed you. It'll take a couple more hours, but you'll be safer."

I set the water on the driver's seat, then turn and hold out my hand.

Doug shakes it and hands me an envelope.

"Oscar Guzman."

I turn the envelope over, then slide it into my back pocket. I want to let Doug know how sorry I am for the way things turned out. He's put a lot of faith in me over the years, and I can't help but feel like I've let him down, like it was all for nothing.

I start to tell him this, but he waves me off and motions to the glove compartment. "I left you something in case you run into any trouble."

I hesitate, then reach in and open the latch. There is a .38 inside, and I stare at it for a moment without speaking.

"It's a good gun," he says. "Hope you never have to use it."

"Me too. Thank you."

"Just keep your eyes open, Jake." He looks over at Diane as she climbs into the passenger seat, then back at me. "I mean it."

- 48 -

By the time we get on the road, the morning traffic is just starting to thin. We pass a couple cop cars on the way out of town, and each time my nerves splinter a little more. It's not until the city is far behind us that I feel myself start to relax.

Diane doesn't.

Every now and then I catch her looking over my shoulder at the speedometer, and I slow down.

She asks if I want her to drive.

"No," I say. "It keeps me calm."

"If we get pulled over—"

"We're not going to get pulled over."

"But if we do—"

"I know."

The words come out harsher than I'd intended, but I don't care. Diane doesn't need to lecture me on what will happen if we're pulled over. We don't have papers on the SUV, and neither of us has a driver's license. My face is bandaged and bruised, and there's a gun in the glove compartment. Any cop would be suspicious.

"It's important, Jake. We need to be careful."

I lean forward and turn on the radio. Diane takes the hint. After a few minutes the sound of the DJ's voice starts to give me a headache, so I shut it off.

I expect Diane to start in again on my driving, but instead she turns toward the passenger window and ignores me.

We drive for several hours in silence.

- - -

I stick to the roads Doug told me about. Most are minor highways, two lanes cutting a wide black gash through the hills and down into the desert. The few cars we see are either dusty, late-model American cars or cattle trucks.

Thirty miles from the border, I slow down and pull over.

"What are you doing?"

"You should drive. We're getting close, and we won't stand out as much if you're behind the wheel."

She opens the passenger door and steps out onto the shoulder. We both walk around to the front of the car, and as she passes me, I reach out and grab her hand.

"No, Jake."

I let her go. "What's wrong?"

"Nothing." She looks up at me, then away. "I'll just feel better when this is done and we're in Mexico. Okay?"

"Okay."

She smiles, then turns and walks the rest of the way around the car to the driver's side. A few minutes later, we're back on the road.

By the time we reach the border, the sun is sitting low on the horizon, and all around us the evening light is warm and orange.

Diane is squeezing the steering wheel tight. I reach over and put my hand on her leg.

"It's going to be fine. Relax."

"Why aren't you nervous? You're the one everyone is looking for."

"I don't know," I say. "I'm just not. Doug told me they don't usually stop people on the way out of the country, just coming in."

"When did he say that?"

"This morning."

"What else did he tell you?"

I think about my conversation with Doug and try to think of something I can share. "He said we should carry extra cash for the police."

"What for?"

"Bribes."

Diane seems to think about this for a moment, then says, "We don't have extra cash."

"No," I say. "So drive slow."

— — —

The first time I see the police and the border guards on the bridge leading into Mexico, I feel a small knot tighten deep in my stomach. It fades when I notice the open gates and empty kiosks.

"Where is everyone?"

I point to the other side of the bridge and the congested northbound traffic. "Looks like they're all over there," I say. "Doug was right."

"And as long as we never come back, we'll be fine."

I don't like the tone of her voice, but I ignore it and look out the window at a group of four border guards standing around two patrol trucks.

They don't look at us as we drive by.

Once we're on the other side, we turn off the bridge and melt into the city traffic.

– – –

Diane stops at a hotel just off the highway and goes inside to get a room for the night. I stay in the car, under the dome light, tracing the route to El Regalo on the map. I use my finger to follow the thin red and blue road lines toward the coast, but my eyes are heavy, and I have to fight to keep them open.

A few minutes later, Diane comes out with a key.

"We got the last room," she says. "They're full."

"We're lucky."

"I don't know. There's a lot of people around here."

She hands me the key then pulls the SUV around to the parking lot behind the building. I take the .38 from the glove compartment and slide it into the back of my belt before we go inside.

The room is like every other hotel room. There's a bed, a desk, and a TV sitting on top of a dresser. The only window is barred and looks out on a chain-link fence and a small square of dying grass littered with trash blown in off the highway.

I close the curtains and turn on the desk lamp.

Diane stands by the door with her arms folded over her chest. She looks at me. "I don't like this."

"It's just for the night."

"I mean stopping," she says. "We should've kept driving. You could've slept in the car."

"What about you?"

"I'm not tired."

"Not yet," I say. "But we have a long way to go. If we leave early tomorrow morning, we'll get there before dark. It'll be fine."

"I don't like it."

I hold out my hand.

Diane hesitates, then takes it. "Do you really think we're safe down here?"

"As safe as anyone is in Mexico, I guess."

"That's not what I meant," she says. "Do you think anyone is going to look for us down here?"

"How could they? No one knows where we are."

"Doug knows."

"He won't say anything."

"Are you sure?"

"Of course I am."

Diane stares at me, then nods. "I'm going to take a bath. You should get some sleep."

I watch her walk into the bathroom and close the door. A few minutes later, I hear the metal scrape of the shower curtain sliding open and water running in the tub.

I set the .38 on the table then sit on the edge of the bed and listen to the hum of the highway outside my window. The noise is loud, and it rolls into the room like the sound of an angry sea.

I reach down to take off my shoes, and my ribs scream at me. I bite down hard against the pain, and once it passes, I inch back on the bed and lie down.

There is a thin brown water stain on the ceiling. I look away and think about Diane, wondering what she's thinking and if she's okay. Part of me wants to stay awake to talk to her, but it's impossible to keep my eyes open.

After a while, I quit trying.

- 49 -

The next morning we wake up early and get back on the road. I drive, and Diane sits in the passenger seat with the map open on her lap. Outside, the day is bright and the air is clear, and the sun shines warm on my skin.

We reach the ocean that afternoon and stop for lunch at a seafood shack on the beach. We take our food out to sit on the sand and stare at the water.

I don't eat right away, and Diane asks me what I'm thinking.

"This is a first for me."

"What is?"

"This." I point out at the blue water and the white waves. "I've never seen the ocean."

"You're kidding."

I shake my head. "I'm not."

Diane smiles, sets her food aside. "So, what do you think of it?"

"It's beautiful."

"Are you going to miss the mountains?"

"Probably, but I'll adapt. How about you?"

"I won't miss them."

"You sound confident."

"There's a trick to never being homesick," she says. "I learned it when I was a kid."

"What's that?"

Diane pauses, says, "Never have a home."

- - -

We drive south for a few more hours, and the view changes from sandy beaches to rocky cliffs to palm forests, thick and green.

Eventually, we pass a sign for El Regalo.

Diane looks down at the map and says, "There should be a turn up here somewhere. Look for a road."

"Don't we need to go into town?"

She holds up the map and points to the line Doug traced for us to follow. "It's before the town."

I don't argue, and when she tells me to turn, I do.

The road is unpaved, and a thick trail of dust lifts into the air behind us as we drive. We pass a line of one-level concrete houses with a group of children playing out front. They stop to watch us go by.

One little girl waves.

I wave back.

The road curves, and then the trees open and I see a haze of blue water in the distance.

"There's the ocean," I say. "The road ends."

Diane doesn't look up from the map. "There's no address. His note says to turn left before we hit the beach, then look for the lawn jockey."

I laugh.

Diane turns to me. "He's not serious, is he?"

"What do you think?"

She shakes her head and mumbles to herself.

The road stops at a line of sand dunes just before the beach, and I turn left in front of a row of stone houses that stretch south along the water. They're bigger than the concrete homes we saw on the way in, but not by much.

Diane says, "Is that it?"

She points to a two-level house with a small, sun-bleached statue out front. It's a man wearing jockey boots and a riding cap and holding a rusted metal ring out in front of him.

"Has to be."

There's no driveway, so I pull off the road and park on the lawn. We get out of the SUV and stretch, staring at the house.

"Doesn't look too bad."

Diane crosses the lawn, past the jockey, and stops at the door. She turns the knob, locked, then walks around to the window. She looks inside, using her hands to shield her eyes from the sun.

"There's furniture in here," she says. "Are you sure this is the place?"

I look around at the other houses. None of them have lawn jockeys out front. I take the key Doug gave me from my pocket and say, "There's only one way to find out."

Diane steps aside, and I slide the key into the lock. It turns easily, and the door opens.

I look at Diane. "I guess this is the place."

- - -

"It's clean." Diane crosses through the room. "When Doug said he hasn't been down here in years, I was thinking the worst."

"I should find the caretaker and tell him we're here." I take the letter Doug gave me before we left out of my back pocket and read the name written on the front. "Oscar Guzman."

"Where is he?"

"He runs the market in town."

Diane nods, then turns and starts wandering around the house. There's not much to it. The main room has two hard couches and a small table with a chess set on top. The kitchen has a sink and a reach-in refrigerator next to a walk-up bar and two stools.

"There's no stove," Diane says. "What kind of house doesn't have a stove?"

I shrug, then walk past her to a set of full-length curtains covering two sliding glass doors. I pull them open, and for a second, I forget to breathe.

I feel Diane come up behind me.

"Oh my God," she says. "It's beautiful."

She's right, it is.

The glass doors open onto a redwood porch and a set of stairs leading down to a thin walking trail that snakes around rocks and over sand dunes toward a rolling line of teal blue water and waves breaking white over white sand.

"You want to go down there?"

"Already?"

I look at Diane. "You have other plans?"

"I thought you wanted to find the caretaker."

"We can walk up the beach into town and introduce ourselves."

"Are you sure you're up for it?"

"The exercise will do me good."

Diane slides the glass door open and steps out.

I follow her.

The breeze coming in off the sea is clean and cool. I breathe deep and taste the salt on my lips.

Diane taps my shoulder and points to the corner of the porch and a large outdoor gas grill. "There's our stove."

I smile. "Mystery solved."

Diane laughs, takes my hand. "Come on, let's go."

I motion to the stairs, and we start down the trail toward the sea.

— — —

Once we reach the ocean, we stop and kick off our shoes. The sand is hot, and Diane skips down to the waterline. She's laughing, and the sound warms me.

The beach is deserted.

I stand on the wet sand, letting the water cover my feet. "Where is everyone?"

"Who cares," Diane says. "I hope it stays like this. I can't wait to go in."

"Not me."

"Why not?"

"I don't swim."

Diane takes my hand. "Maybe I can change that."

I laugh. "Maybe you can."

We start walking south toward town, stopping every few feet to pick up a shell or piece of driftwood to throw back into the sea. The sun is burning low on the horizon, reflecting a rusted line of fire across the surface of the water, all the way to the shore.

I put my arm around Diane's shoulder. "I think I could get used to this."

She looks down at her feet as she walks, silent.

"You know, this could be a new start," I say. "We can put everything behind us and go back to the beginning."

"You think so?"

"Why not?"

Diane smiles, then steps closer and leans into me as we walk. "Let's just wait and see."

I don't like her answer, but I let it go.

We walk for a while longer. The closer we get to town, the more houses we see along the coast. A few are white and modern, but most are older. These are dark and weatherworn, and they blend in to the dunes, hidden by sand and trees.

There is a wooden signpost dug into the beach up ahead. We passed another one by the house, but I'd been distracted by the view and didn't pay attention.

Now, looking up and down the coast, I notice several identical signs, each one spaced about a hundred yards apart.

I stop and read the words stenciled in green spray paint across the front.

"*Ninguna Natacion!*"

Then under it.

"*Corriente de Resaca!*"

Diane is next to me, reading over my shoulder.

"What does it say?"

"It says we can't swim." She pauses, frowns. "There's a riptide. The currents are too strong."

I turn and look out at the ocean. The water is so blue and so beautiful that it's hard to believe it could be dangerous.

We keep walking, but now we're both quiet.

After a little while, Diane stops and says, "I think I want to go back. I'm tired."

I stop and look down the beach toward the town.

"Are you sure?" I ask. "We're almost there."

"You go ahead," she says. "I'll meet you."

I could keep going, but the sound of her voice, distant and detached, worries me.

I decide we've gone far enough.

"This can wait," I say. "Let's go back."

Diane smiles and reaches for my hand.

We turn and walk back down the beach together.

– 50 –

The next day we drive into El Regalo and introduce ourselves to Oscar Guzman at the town market. He's older than I expected, and he watches us closely as we talk, as if he's expecting us to steal something.

It's not until I mention Doug's name that his eyes grow wide and he smiles, grand and welcoming, showing a thin scatter of yellow teeth.

"Mr. Doug?"

I take the letter from my pocket and hand it over. Oscar looks at it like it's dirty and drops it unread on a stack of wooden vegetable crates next to his chair.

"How long?"

I look at Diane. "How long what?"

She says something to him in Spanish, and he answers.

"He wants to know how long we're going to be at the house," she says. "He wants to know if Doug will keep sending him money while we're here."

"Tell him I'll make sure he does."

Diane tells him, and Oscar smiles. He reaches out and shakes my hand, talking fast. I can't understand a word, but Diane follows along without a problem.

She translates as she listens.

"He says the roof leaks in the front of the house, and not to use the outside shower."

"There's an outside shower?"

"He says it's next to the porch, and it's for rinsing off after swimming." She listens. "And it's broken."

"We can't go in the water anyway," I say. "Ask him about the signs on the beach."

Diane asks, and when she finishes talking, Oscar points west toward the water and shakes his finger in the air, as if scolding a child. "*Natacion.*"

I nod. "I know, the riptide."

"*Si.*" He nods. "*Tiburones.*"

I look at Diane.

Oscar leans forward and slaps his hands together in front of me, one on top of the other. He laughs, then does it again, making a loud chomping noise each time.

I step back.

Oscar smiles, says something to Diane.

I wait for her to translate.

"He says the water will carry you out to the sharks." She pauses, listens. "And he thinks he scared you."

"He didn't."

She looks at me, her eyes reflecting the light. "You did jump."

"I think he's crazy." I tap the side of my head, then point to him and say, "Loco."

Oscar laughs, loud and rolling, then takes a brown paper bag from a shelf next to his chair and fills it with avocados. He hands the bag to me and says, in perfect English, "Welcome to El Regalo."

- - -

That evening, I'm sitting on the porch watching the sunset when Diane comes out carrying a cardboard box.

"Look what I found." She sets the box on the ground at my feet and opens the top flaps. "Books, lots of them, and there are three or four more boxes in the closet."

I reach down and take one out. The pages are yellow with age, and the cover is missing. I turn it around and read the name on the spine.

"Day Keene?" I drop the book back in the box then grab a few more and read the names. "Fredric Brown, Ed Lacy, Horace McCoy."

"Have you heard of them?"

"Some of them," I say. "These are really old."

"But they're in good shape," Diane says. "Readable, at least."

I pick up another and flip through the pages.

"What's that one?"

I look at the spine, say, "James M. Cain."

"Do you know it?"

I tell her I do, then lean back and open to the first page.

— — —

For the next couple weeks, things are good. Diane and I spend most of our time sitting around the house, reading Doug's collection of pulp paperbacks, or walking along the beach. The days are peaceful, my body is healing, and for a while I let myself relax and believe everything is normal.

We don't talk about what happened back home, and I don't push the subject. I still keep Doug's .38 on the bedside table, and she doesn't say a word about it.

Things have changed.

Sometimes I'll catch her staring up at the sky or out at the water, lost in thought, and I'll ask what's on her mind. Usually she doesn't answer, but if she does, it's always the same thing.

She asks me if I think Gabby is looking for us.

I tell her he's not, and I believe it.

Most of the time this helps, and Diane will come back from whatever dark place she's in, and things will be good again for a while.

Other times it doesn't help at all.

"How do you know?"

"If he was looking for us, he'd have found us by now."

This stops her, and I see her struggling to find the words. "No one knows we're here but Doug."

"That's right."

"You said he wouldn't tell anyone."

"He won't," I say. "But Gabby is different. If he really wanted to find us, he'd find us."

Diane turns away and walks to the glass doors. She looks out at the ocean, arms folded across her chest. "I don't think I can take this much longer."

"Take what?"

"Not knowing."

I don't say anything.

She looks back at me. "Will you do something for me?"

"What?"

"Call Doug," she says. "Find out what's going on, see if he's heard anything."

"I can't," I say. "I told him I wouldn't call for at least a month. It's only been a few weeks."

"Please, Jake. I need to know." I can hear the tears behind her voice, getting closer to the surface with each word. "Every time a car passes, my heart starts racing so fast that I think it's going to explode."

"And calling Doug is going to make it better?"

"I think I saw a pay phone up the street," she says. "You can call from there."

"If I call, I'll go into town this afternoon and call from the market," I say. "But I think it's a mistake."

Diane stares at me, then says, "Are you mad at me?"

I shake my head and tell her I'm not, but we both know it's a lie.

— — —

I'm standing outside the market holding the phone against my ear with my shoulder while I sort through a handful of coins, dropping them in the slot. When I've deposited enough money, I dial Doug's number and wait.

The phone rings.

It sounds a million miles away.

I start thinking about what I'll say when Doug answers. Nothing comes to me, and I can feel myself getting more and more angry with each ring. I realize that Doug put himself at risk to help us, and that calling him now, just to make Diane feel better, could be dangerous.

That thought is all it takes. I hang up after the third ring. I stare at the phone for a while, then turn and walk inside the shop to buy some fruit to take home.

Oscar is arranging tomatoes in a wooden crate. He sees me and nods. "Hello, Jake. Just you today?"

"Just me." I can feel my bad mood spreading, covering me like a cloud passing in front of the sun. "What's good today?"

"Everything, my friend." Oscar holds up one of the tomatoes for me to see. "You like?"

"Sure," I say. "I'll take a couple."

He picks out a few of the best ones and sets them on the counter in front of me. Then he touches his forehead with his fingers and says, "I have something else for you."

I tell him I don't need anything else, that the tomatoes are fine, but he waves me off and disappears behind a curtain in the back of the store.

For a second, I think about leaving money on the counter and walking out, but I can't bring myself to do it.

A few minutes later, Oscar comes out with a package. It's about the size of a shoebox, and it's wrapped in white butcher paper. He sets it next to the tomatoes.

"This came yesterday." His voice drops to a whisper. "A private courier. It's addressed to you."

I feel something inside me drop away.

I turn the box around on the counter, and read the shipping label. I recognize the handwriting immediately.

"Are you okay?"

I look up at Oscar. "This came yesterday?"

He nods.

"Do you have a knife?"

Oscar takes a small paring knife from behind the counter and hands it to me. I use it to cut the tape away from the package, then I open the box and look inside. There's a yellow Post-it note sitting on top. I pick it up and read.

"Something important?" Oscar asks.

I crumple the note and slide it into my pocket. "A gift," I say. "From an old friend."

- 51 -

I tell Oscar I've changed my mind about the tomatoes and ask for a bottle of whiskey instead.

He sells it to me without a word.

When I get home, I set the package on the counter, take a glass from the cabinet and pour myself a drink.

Diane is sitting outside on the porch with a book open on her lap. When she hears me, she stands in the doorway and says, "What did he say?"

"I didn't call him."

"What?" She slaps the book closed. "Why not?"

"It wasn't the right thing to do," I say. "Doug is involved in this, too, and I don't want to get him in any more trouble than he's already in."

"But—"

I pick up the glass and take a drink.

"And now you're drinking again?"

"That's right," I say. "I'm drinking again."

Diane crosses the room to the bar. When she sees the package she stops. "What's this?"

"It was delivered to the market," I say. "Oscar signed for it."

"Did you open it?"

I nod, take another drink.

"Who sent it?"

"Gabby."

Diane raises one hand to her mouth. She sets her book on the bar and walks around to the counter, slow. "He knows we're here?"

"It looks that way."

"What is it?"

"Open it, see for yourself."

Diane pulls the box toward her, lifts the top, and looks inside. "Oh my God."

I turn away and pour another drink.

Diane is silent.

"There was a note."

"Where is it?"

I take the crumpled yellow Post-it out of my pocket and read, *"I'm sorry, Jake. Gabby."*

"He's sorry?" Diane takes the note from me. "That's all it says?"

"That's all."

She flips the note over and checks the back, then drops it next to the package. "What do you think?"

"I don't know."

Diane turns back to the box. She reaches inside and lifts out the dove statue. Then she sets it on the counter and runs her hands over the surface. "My God, it's still sealed."

I take another drink.

"Do you see what this is?" She looks at me, her eyes wide, glowing. "He's trying to make amends. He knows he made a mistake, and he wants to make it up to you."

"I don't think so."

"What else could it be?"

I tell her I don't know, and it's the truth.

I reach for the bottle to pour another drink, and then I feel Diane's hand on top of mine, stopping me.

"Don't," she says. "Not tonight."

I set the bottle down.

"Don't you see? We're free." She leans forward and kisses me. "It's over."

I start to tell her that the police might see things differently back home, but then I notice the way she's looking at me, and the words don't come out.

She kisses me again, then takes my hand and leads me back to the bedroom. For the moment, nothing else matters.

– – –

That night, lying next to Diane and staring up at the ceiling fan as it moves hot air through the room, I try to think of all the reasons Gabby might've sent the statue.

I know that everything he does, he does for a reason, but I can't figure this one out.

What bothers me most is the note.

I tell myself it's possible that Diane is right, and that Gabby sent the bird as an apology, but in all the years I've known him, I've never once heard Gabby say he was sorry. The idea that he'd start now just doesn't make sense.

There has to be another reason.

I stay awake for a long time, going over every possibility. When sleep finally comes, it covers me like a wave, dark and dreamless.

- - -

When I wake up the next morning, I'm alone.

I sit up then slip on my pants and walk out to the kitchen. I take a bottle of water from the refrigerator and drink half of it, then cross the living room to the sliding glass doors and look out at the ocean.

I don't see Diane.

I finish the water, then set the empty bottle on the bar and call her name. There's no answer, so I open the glass doors and step outside. Diane isn't on the porch, but there are two couch pillows on the floor in the corner.

I walk over and pick them up.

The dove statue is lying underneath, broken and empty.

- - -

Both the .38 and the SUV are gone, so I walk down the path to the beach and head south into town. Once I get there, I go into the market and ask Oscar if he's seen Diane.

"Not today," Oscar says. "Is she coming in?"

I tell him I don't know, then describe the SUV and ask if he's seen it around town.

He shakes his head. "No, I'm sorry."

I brush it off, say, "She'll show up. We're celebrating tonight."

Oscar smiles, then reaches behind the counter and pulls out a bottle of red wine. He hands it to me. "For your celebration?"

I smile. "I'll take it."

Before I leave, I buy two steaks, several peppers, and another bottle of whiskey to go along with the wine. Oscar puts it all in a white canvas bag and hands it to me over the counter. I thank him, then walk out into the sunlight.

On my way home, I stop at the pay phone and call Doug. I let the phone ring several times, but he doesn't answer.

I hang up and dial his office number.

I'm not sure what day it is, but when he doesn't answer his office phone, I tell myself that he's probably in class, and there's no reason to worry.

I don't leave a message.

I slip the bag's canvas strap over my shoulder and walk down to the beach. On the way home, I stop and sit next to one of the wooden no-swimming signs and watch the sunlight reflect white off the surface of the water.

I stay there for a long time, letting the image burn into me. Then I take the whiskey bottle from the bag, break the seal, and drink.

– – –

Diane still isn't back that afternoon.

I wait until evening, and then I take the steaks and peppers out to the grill to cook. I stand over them with a spatula in one hand and the open wine bottle in the other while the sun drops below the horizon and the sky above me burns itself black.

When the steaks are done, I put them on two plates and set them on the kitchen table. I finish mine, then switch plates and eat Diane's, too, washing them down with the rest of the wine.

I stack the plates on top of each other and drop them in the sink. Then I grab the whiskey bottle and go back to the table.

A minute later, someone knocks at the door.

At first I think it's my imagination, and I don't move. Then the knocking comes again, louder this time.

I push myself up and start down the hallway toward the front of the house.

I slide the bolt lock and open the door.

Gabby is standing outside with an older man I don't recognize. Gabby smiles, the other one doesn't.

"Hello, Jake," he says. "You sure are a hard man to find."

– 52 –

I don't move, and for a while we just stand there on the front porch, staring at each other.

Then Gabby motions past me and says, "Can we talk?"

"She's gone," I say. "If that's why you're here."

"I know she's gone, and no, that's not why I'm here." He pauses. "You going to let me in or not?"

I hesitate, then step back, holding the door.

Gabby walks in first, looking around the living room as he does. The other man follows.

"You've been down here this whole time?"

"How'd you find me?"

"Not important." He snaps his fingers and points. "Did you get the gift?"

"Was that what it was?"

"Depends how you look at it," he says. "I think I did you a favor and showed you her true colors. That sounds like a gift to me."

I think about the note and the apology. All at once, everything clicks into place. Gabby had to be right. He knew what would happen when he sent the statue, and he knew what Diane would do when she saw the diamonds. This was his way of proving to me that he was right about her all along.

He wasn't apologizing for what he'd done back home. He was apologizing for what he knew was coming, what he knew she'd do.

"You knew what was going to happen."

"It wasn't hard to figure out, kid. You were just too close to see her for what she was."

Even faced with the facts, a part of me still doesn't believe it's true. A part of me still believes she loved me, that not all of it was a lie. But this time, I keep that part of me quiet.

"Like I said, she's not here." I walk past them and into the kitchen. "She took the diamonds, and I don't know where she is."

They follow me.

"We know," Gabby says. "But don't worry about that. We'll get to her. Tonight, I'm here to see you."

The tone of his voice is cold and feels like a frost crawling along my spine. I reach down and take the whiskey bottle off the table and drink.

I tell myself I won't be afraid.

Gabby walks to the sliding glass doors and looks out at the darkness. He doesn't speak.

"So what do you want?" I take another drink. "Did you come to thank me for saving your life?"

Gabby laughs, then turns around and looks at me. "That's right, Jake. That's exactly why I'm here." He puts a hand on my shoulder and pats my cheek with the other. "Thank you."

I look down at the bottle in my hand, but I don't think I have the strength to lift it.

"This is a nice place." Gabby looks at the old man standing along the wall, then points to the glass doors. "Did you see how close we are to the water?"

The old man shakes his head, doesn't speak.

"Is it easy to get down there?"

I feel my stomach twist. I nod, silent.

"Well, come on then, show me the way. I love the ocean at night."

My legs feel weak, but I manage to walk over to the table and set the whiskey bottle down. I motion to the doors leading out onto the porch. "After you."

"You lead the way," Gabby says. "It's your house."

I pull the doors open, and we all walk out onto the porch and down the steps to the long path leading to the sea. There are no stars tonight, just the full moon, cold and bright against a depthless black sky.

When we get to the water, I stop and let the waves roll in over my feet. Gabby stands next to me, and we stay there for a long time, staring out at the reflection of the moon on the ocean.

The sea is loud, and I focus on the sound until the world drops away and that's all that's left.

A few minutes pass. Then Gabby turns and looks at me. "We can't stay, Jake."

"I know."

"I wish you would've trusted me." He shakes his head. "Things could've been different."

I don't look at him, just stare out at the moon and listen to the roar of the sea. "They are what they are."

Gabby frowns. "You're right about that."

He looks past me and nods to the man standing behind us, then he puts his hands on my shoulders and squeezes.

He lets go and walks away.

Behind me, the old man steps closer.

I close my eyes and focus on the sound of the sea.

I tell myself I'm not afraid, but I still jump when I hear the gunshot.

It takes a minute before I realize I'm still standing.

I hear movement behind me, and when I turn around, the old man is lying on the ground. Blood is blooming out from a hole in his shirt, soaking into the cloth. He claws at the sand, once, then stops and doesn't move again.

Gabby is looking back toward the house, shifting his weight from one foot to the other, trying to decide which way to go. I follow his gaze and see Diane walking down the beach from the path. She has Doug's .38, and she's aiming it at Gabby.

As she gets closer, he turns to me and laughs.

"Jake?"

Then Diane pulls the trigger.

– – –

"Come on," Diane says. "Help me."

She hands me the .38 then bends down and lifts the old man's legs. Gabby is lying facedown a few feet away, and I can't take my eyes off him.

"Help me."

I slip the .38 into the back of my belt, then come around and lift the old man's shoulders. Together we drag him into the surf and float him out as far as we can.

Even in a few feet of water, the current is strong.

It pulls at us as we walk back to shore.

Diane runs over to Gabby's body and tries to turn him onto his back. I follow her, slow.

"We have to hurry," she says. "What are you doing?"

I can't think of what to say, so I start with the obvious question. "Where were you?"

Diane takes a breath, and I see her shoulders drop. "Can we do this later?"

"I want to know."

"I left," she says. "I stayed up all night thinking about that note and wondering why he sent you the statue. The more I thought about it, the more I knew he was coming, so I took the diamonds and the gun and hid from him, and from you."

"Why?"

"Because he wanted to kill us, that's why." She holds out her hands. "This was the only plan that would work. He expected me to leave, so he had to think I did."

"But why didn't you tell me?" I ask. "Why did you just leave without a word?"

"You would've tried to talk me out of it, and I would've let you." She looks up and smiles. "I couldn't do that this time. I knew I was right."

I can't argue with her, and I don't.

Instead I say, "Why did you come back?"

Diane's eyes go wide, and she smiles. "Why do you think I came back?" She shakes her head and laughs under her breath. "I love you, Jake."

A few seconds pass. Diane grabs Gabby's shoulder and tries again to turn him over. "Will you give me a hand, please?"

I get down next to her and we push him over onto his back. When we do, he stares up at us, his mouth opening and closing, silent.

"Jesus," I say. "He's still alive."

Diane ignores me. She walks around and lifts his legs, then nods toward his head. "Come on, we have to do this."

"But he's still alive."

"Pick him up."

I hesitate, then grab Gabby's shoulders. We drag him down the beach toward the water. Gabby is whispering something, but the sea is loud, and his words are lost in the sound.

We push him out into the surf and let the tide take him. Then Diane and I stand at the edge of the water and watch as the currents pull him away from the shore.

Silent.

After a few minutes, I ask, "Now what?"

"What do you mean?"

"Where do we go from here?"

"Anywhere we want," she says. "We're free."

Somewhere, far from shore, I think I hear Gabby crying out to me. I tell myself it's just the wind.

Diane steps closer and leans into me.

I slide my arm around her shoulders, and we stand like that for a long time, staring out at the sea.

"I love you, Jake. Do you know that?"

I look down and see her eyes, clear and bright in the moonlight. It makes me smile.

"Yeah," I say. "I do."

ACKNOWLEDGMENTS

I'd like to thank my agent, Allan Guthrie, for his advice and his patience. Thank you to my editors, Terry Goodman at Thomas & Mercer, and Francesca Main at Simon & Schuster. Thanks to my early readers, Kurt Dinan, John Mantooth, Eric Smetana, John Hornor Jacobs, Stephen Sommerville, and Sean Doolittle for their time, their generosity, and their invaluable insight during the early drafts of this novel. I'd also like to express my sincere gratitude to Jeff Belle, Sarah Tomashek, Jacque Ben Zekry, David Downing, and everyone on the Thomas & Mercer team for their hard work, their passion, and their unmatched dedication to their books and their authors. Most of all, I'd like to thank my wife, Amy, for her love and her support, and for believing when I didn't.

ABOUT THE AUTHOR

 John Rector is a prize-winning short story writer and the author of the novels *The Grove* and *The Cold Kiss*, which was named Best Debut Novel of 2010 by *Suspense Magazine* and optioned for a feature film currently in development.